CLOSE

Personal...

Poetically

Speaking

By William Gray

Up Close and Personal... Poetically Speaking

Published by William Gray

Please send comments and questions:

William Gray

15802 Mission Estates Ct Houston TX 77083

Printed in the United States of America.

ISBN: 978-1-945066-00-9

ISBN: E-Book: 978-0-9971378-3-5

Library Control # 2016918197

Contents:

America, Bless God 7
The Fallen Star 11
Burn Out 13
My Hero..."The Forgotten One" 14
Time for Change 17
Death Row "The Life You Choose" 19
Just Say No...My Testimony 20
Slipping Into Darkness (A Testimony) 23
Soldier's Story 25
Evil Among You 28
Menace to Society (A doomed Breed) 30
Last Call 32
It Ain't Safe...To Die! 35
An Invasion on Earth 37
Running Scared. "The Day of the Lord" 40
Like Father Like Son (The Curse) 42
Evil Among You..."Ain't Nobody Listening" 44
My Pastor "Anthony Mosley" 46
Jesus...A Bridge Over Troubled Waters 47
Psalms 49
Lifestyles 50
Play No Games 52
Peace Be Still 53
The Home Boys "No Limit Soldiers" 54
Where Would I Be 56
The Enemy (Prelude) 58
The Enemy 59
Move...Get Out The Way 61
Goodbye Satan "The Letter" 63

Goodbye, Old Man 64
Let the Truth be Told, Not Sold 66
It's Time 68
Coming Out of Tradition 69
Do You Remember... 72
My daughter 74
In Memory of Michelle Y. Gray... "She will be Missed." 75
Facing T.D.C Texas Department of Corrections 76
The Last Harvest 78
A Time to Fear 80
Pray, Without Ceasing 82
A Safe Place...in Jesus 84
Don't Be Stupid! 86
Unprotected 89
The Hemphill Story 93
Caught Up 96
You've Tried the Rest...Now Try the Best! 100
Alpha and Omega (The Beginning, The End, The First, The last) 103
Watchha Gonna Do 105
The Preacher 109
They Shall Know "I am the Lord" 112
The Love of a Baby Sister...We Never had a Clue 115
Bow Down 116
About the Author 117

Dedication

This book is dedicated to The Gray Family with special dedication to my sisters Michele Y. Gray and Brenda Reed. A special Holla' to Lil Sis Brenda. Thank you on behalf of Fam. God bless John James, Brian, Watasa Ohijai, Unc. LUVs you.

Dedication

[illegible]

America, Bless God!

Caller dials 911... Dispatcher: What's your emergency?
Caller: America has forsaken their God.

There are so many things that occur and take place in this world today. Things we sometimes cannot understand in the natural. Each and everyday the earth suffers a disaster in some form or fashion. Strange occurrences, death, destruction, unusual happenings, and phenomenon's. Some would think these occurrences are the works of the devil, denoted in the popular term, "The devil is busy." There are those who might also say, "God is tired." To be perfectly honest God is tired. He is tired of His children being disobedient, rebellious, and most of all He's tired of us refusing to acknowledge Him and His commands.

I believe God is tired of being forsaken. How can man overlook or forget God, the Most High? We do, however, and when death and destruction comes upon us, we ask, "Why Lord, why? Lord, I go to church, I pay my tithes. I'm a good person Lord, why?" I can say one thing, "Something's hidden are because they're forbidden." We're not being honest with God and ourselves. God is tired America. Jeremiah 16:17-18:
"For mine eyes are upon all their ways; They are not hid from My Face, neither is their iniquity hid from mine eyes, and first I will recompense their iniquity and their sin double; because they have defiled my land. They have filled my inheritance with the carcasses of their detestable and abominable things."

The great US of A in all her splendor, her wealth, the Land of the Free, the home of the brave.... is digging her own grave. Believe it or not, people are literally dying to be a part of this great country. America we really don' t know how blessed we are. God has blessed this country to be a land flowing with milk and honey. He has blessed us all through first given us life, and what appreciation do we extend? We refuse to acknowledge Him in Word or in deed. To this day we have the audacity to ask God to Bless America!

Jeremiah 9:9, "Shall I not visit them for these things? Saith the Lord; shall not my soul be avenged on such a nation as this?" America, God has done His part and blessed you we must do our part and not forget to "Bless God." Americans can believe in the lie that by their mind, hands and power were they able to obtain such wealth. "Oh child, I worked 50 years to get what I have." "Oh, but who gave you power, strength, life, that you are able to work and accomplish those things? Does not this God deserve to be blessed? Bless the Lord oh my soul and all that is within me, I will bless His Holy Name!

Why do we refuse to acknowledge Christ Jesus, the gift, and wisdom of His holiness? We as Americans continue to ask God to bless us and because He's merciful, God does just that. He blesses us then when He does, we forget about Him. I'm a living witness God delivered me countless times from the hands of the enemy and when He did I forgot the Lord as billions of others had. My question is, "How long will God continue to bless America as we forsake and forget Him?" Even though we get numerous warnings we still forget and not turn to bless Him.

Deut. 8:11-20, Beware that we forget not the Lord our God, who led us through that great and terrible wilderness. Who fed us while in our wilderness and multiplied our herds, silver, and gold. He gave us good land to grow on. But when we have eaten and are full, our heart can be lifted up and forget the Lord God who brought us forth out of Egypt. If we do forget the Lord our God and walk after other gods, serve them, worship them, He testified against us that we shall surely perish.

The Bible says in Deuteronomy 8:10 that we should bless the Lord our God for the good land which He has given us. "America!" Verse 20 tells us, "As the nations which the Lord destroyed before your face so shall ye perish." America because we are not obedient unto the voice of the Lord our God, destruction is near.

Believe me, God is trying desperately to get our attention. I know this may seem hard to some but it's the truth and God wants us to hear the 911 call!

The World Trade Centers, sure it was a tragic situation, but we have to realize God holds the keys to life and death. We want God to bless us, but yet we worship idol gods, glorify the flag, praise the heroes, when we should recognize the cross from which our savior hung; and the blood stained banner on which His blood was shed that we as Americans could have eternal life. It's sad after this devastating disaster, the sales of the flag sky rocketed in sale, t-shirts bearing logos such as, "God Bless America" did likewise along with, "The Pride of America" and so forth. Our priorities are not in perspective and believe me, God is about fed up with our unfaithfulness.

Jer. 22:6-9 says, "For this saith the Lord unto the Kings house of Judah; Thou art Gilead unto me, and the head of Lebanon; yet surely I will make thee a wilderness, and cities, which are not inhabited. And I will prepare destroyers against thee everyone with his weapons; and they shall cut down thy choice cedars and cast them into the fire." Reminds me of 9/11 and the Trade Centers, America's choice cedars. The Twin Towers.

It's time to Bless God and stop taking matters into our own hands. Consult God and receive His divine guidance. Certainly the New York incident was a devastating event and it drew worldwide attention; which is exactly what God wants from you. Attention! God is a jealous God, Bless Him America. Church Bless His Holy Name. The Bible says, "You will bless Him, Every knee shall bow and every tongue confess!" Its time to get focused America before its too late. God is pleading with us to turn from our wicked ways and began to bless, worship, and praise Him. The Lord has given us the gift of life; but just like he gave, he can also take away. He brought us unto this earth surely He can take us out!

Bless God America for He is worthy. Bless God America for His Son Jesus Christ. Keep looking to the flag...old glory for salvation. Keep worshiping that which profit not, keep forsaking the Lord your God. Keep denying Him and you'll see, 911, you'll find your self in a state of emergency.

Amen

Yes, the devastating earthquake in Haiti will be a time to remember, but bless God America and begin sending up your timber and praises. Amen.

The Fallen Star

During the course of my life and through many teachings and experiences I've come to know that Satan is really real and definitely alive. I've also come to know that he wasn't always the way he is today. He was actually good in God's eyes and was highly favored. He was God's number one angel, well until he started having other ideas to over throw The Creator; absurd!

In heaven, Satan was a star, the star of dawn. He was a star that fell from grace as if God had said to him, "Get to hell and out of my face!" Literally, because when He kicked him out of heaven, hell would be his headquarters.

Looking at that picture I consider my life. There were times when I found myself like Satan, not knowing that the good things that took place in my life were not of my doing, but of God. The Lord blessed me at my release from prison with a very good job, a wife, a home and two fine cars. I had money in the bank. In all actuality I had favor with God; that is until I got the "Big Head." I did not acknowledge God for all my accomplishments—my blessings; I thought it was all me.

I thought I was all that and a bag of chips, but as time went on, I found my blessings slowly diminishing. My fame turned into shame. I was dwindling to nothing. I lost everything and even worst I resorted to drugs and alcohol. I was cast down to a living hell. I was as Satan, "The fallen star." I became miserable and I wanted to make everyone else's life miserable too.

I was chained and in bondage. I wanted to kill, steal, and destroy but I've come to know today, I don't have to be a fallen star. I can repent and acknowledge Christ Jesus and again find favor with God. Unlike Satan, he had his opportunity and blew it!

You were and angel of beauty, God made you, you had special duty.
You wore the best of jewels you were of splendor.
Now because of your pride, you only hinder those who choose not the things you do.
You had the seal of perfection you were of God, you needed no correction.
You were of wisdom and perfect in every way.
You went against God, which deprived you of your stay.
God created you and made you of high rank, a cover, you were the anointed cherub you were above all others.
You were on the holy mountain you walked in the midst of stones of fire.
You were of God His hearts desire. But because He gave you favor your heart was lifted up.
You became high minded, beautiful, and then corrupt.
God would no longer tolerate your corruption so there was a shake in the heaven, a violent eruption. You, your army yes had to leave, and now you're in the earth and many you deceive.
O foolish one, you had it made and now you're angry and want to get paid.
To steal souls now; with you it's a must, but it's in God do we put our trust.
It's not our fault the way you are...Lucifer, Satan, the fallen star.

Burn Out

Boilermakers, manufacturers, children of God, continue to wait on the coming of the Lord. Though some will say that it has been years, since the coming of Jesus, but believe me it is coming a day when some will tire out. tTe living, the dead in Christ?" Is He coming back to uphold the sacrifice?"

Be steadfast; I say to you in the Word of God. Don't be bored as to the coming of the Lord and getting to the point where faith is shut out. Denying the love of Christ because of a "burn out." If you're in Christ and He is in you, you'll watch, fight, and pray, like He told you to. Be strong in the Lord and stay in the Word so when He does return you'll be caught up in the Holy Herd. "Your partitions to God will have been heard."

There was a time and will come a time for dispensation when God will deal with His creation. Those who *Burn Out* on the Lord and His coming, Satan is calling and it's you he's summoning. When we go through life with repeated matters, especially in Jesus, we're only climbing the ladder.

Until He returns, be spiritually fed. Stay in church, praise and shout; believe in Christ and don't burn out. Because those that burn out and give up on Christ, the day will come when they'll pay the price. So take a profound look into the living Word, The Second coming is scripture and is God's Word. If He's done it once, He'll do it again. It's best we think of how it all began.

Be burned out if your faith is weak, but there's a small still voice, and you should hear him speak. For the day will come when the sky will split and the trumpets will sound, informing you, our Lord Jesus is Coming Down. Amen!

My Hero... "The Forgotten One"

I'm reminded today of the seriousness of souls being saved. For today the world has lost focus of reality. They have placed their priorities in those things, which do not profit them one iota. Their values are materialistic, they worship idols; they look for heroes...here on earth.

When I see these things, my heart saddens and I'm again reminded of how God used Moses to lead the People of Israel out of the hands of the enemy who sought to do them harm. Pharaoh had purposed in his heart to destroy these people.

God, being who He is had compassion for these people. These people whom He loved, were considered His chosen ones. He saved them, something a hero does if I'm not mistaken. And what gratitude did they show? They went and made a golden calf, and worshiped it and made it their god. This grieved God and made Him very angry.

Today the world has not changed and it's nothing new to God. The Bible says, "For there is nothing new under the sun." God is leading those who wish to be led. He is protecting us loving us providing for us instructing us and what do we do? We continue to look for a hero.

September 11, 2001 America was asked whom do they think or what face should appear on the magazine of Newsweek, who did they consider to be a hero, during this disaster? Their choice was..."The Fire Fighters."

My friends we today live in a confused society. We look for love in all the wrong places. When love is just a whisper a way. Jesus. The unsung Hero. Yes, the world is confused. They feel America is the most powerful country in the world, they feel they cannot be touched, but the Bible tells me there is no weapon formed that could prosper... Just those words alone should make one stop and think. And then, I read in Jeremiah were God said, I will prepare destroyers against you and your weapons.

Now, someone with this kind of power can be my hero any day, any time, any place. Not superman, batman, Spiderman, "A fire man." Don't get me wrong, thank God for firemen. God uses them too, but to consider him a hero over God is ludicrous. Just think about it. When the Great Fire comes who will be your hero then? Will it be the firefighter?

I think not; because if his heart is not with Jesus he will be too busy fighting the fire off himself. Tell me, whom will you rely on for deliverance? Who will you look to for salvation? Who will be your hero, to deliver you from hell after judgment? We live in a confused society. This is a society where prayer is on the back burner of most people's hearts.

My friends, there are only 3 heroes in this life and these 3 are 1 in Jesus Christ. The only hero in this world, the only face to appear across the minds and hearts of this nation. Jesus Christ...the Lord of Lords, host of hosts, king of kings...hero of heroes. The one who took on the sins of men, who took on the sins of the world that we could have life eternal, down at the cross, He became my hero.

Tell me who is the real hero? He is the one the world does not recognize and have neglected, denied and failed to rely on; and that's because of their lifestyles. Another subject God will give me to expound on but it hurts; however to know people feel the way they do about someone who truly loves them. This is really, really, sad and not only does it make me angry, it makes God angry; let me tell you what He proposes to do about it.

Remember how His Word does not return void? Zephaniah 3:8-9, "There fore, wait for me says the Lord until the day I rise up for plunder. My determination is to gather the nations to my assembly of kingdoms to pour on them my indignation all my fierce anger all the earth shall be devoured with the fire of my jealousy. For then

I will restore to the people a pure language that they all may call on the name of the Lord to serve him."

He is a true Hero; that will have us all worship with one accord. God has brought to my mind a married couple. The husband did all he could to please his wife. He provided riches and whatever she wanted. He protected her, loved her, and was her hero. But as time went on, she was deceived and thought that there was another greater hero; whom I elect to call a zero.

This zero was far greater than all she ever knew. She ventured out leaving her true hero, which led to a life of disaster, humiliation, exploitation, and divorce. A separation from God, her covering, that choice made her life go downhill. It sadden her husband, made him bitter, angry, he wept. Jesus wept. And now I weep, every time I think of the cruelness of this world.

I don't know about you but when I find myself in the pits and can't seem to get out; caught up and facing a horrifying situation. Finding myself trapped by the enemy, fighting for my life. I remind myself to pray, laying at the feet of my hero. My Lord and my Savior Jesus Christ. Amen.

Time for Change

I know coming from me this may sound strange but I feel in my heart its now time for changes considering all the times that I 've went astray. I would hear that small still voice reminding me of a better way.

I've found that I can't continue living the life I led, not if I plan to ever get ahead. I now have the opportunity to check with the master, and He's given me the antidote to free me from disaster.

Come to church and receive the Word from my Pastor, stay in God's will, and when the trials and tribulations come... "Peace, Be Still!" Now all this is good and does have its substance, but there's plans for you also and life in abundance.

I know I'm a strong man, a man of might, and I know in my heart I can do right. It's time now for me to settle down and make positive plans and it would mean a lot to me to know just where you stand. I know its up to me, my life to rearrange, and I know in your heart you felt it's "Time for a change." I look back on the times when you would often say, "You do some jacked up stuff, and it's going to catch up with you one day. That day has come and I do have a testimony to tell but let me admonish you because you know me so very well."

It's time for me to focus on what it is I must do, but most importantly I must start listening to my Pastor, and of course you. I know you mean me well and you love me a lot but if I don't make that change that love for me could stop.

Now this is something I could not allow or could never be. We've had too many wonderful moments for you to just set me free. Although Pastor says, "You're not going anywhere, it's still up to me to find my place of there.

So I thank God Today for blessing me with you, I thank him for your love, prayers, and faithfulness so true.

I thank him for your seeing and staying through thick and thin. I thank him for a change in me that will never end. Amen.

Death Row "The Life You Choose"

Darkness comes… there is no light
The sky splits, the Trumpet sounds, the people take flight,
The locust are loosed; they have devoured the land
Cities are desolate and life has ceased, in that of man
Living in fear afraid of what is to come
Because of Capital crimes you have done
Forsaking the Father; and going through life on your own
Death Row… the Executioners song
Living in sin and refusing to repent
The Lord diligently reaches out, his Son He sent
The option being yours and you refuse
Death Row, the life you choose
A life of imprisonment, in bondage; in hell
It's Death Row, my friends, Satan's holding cell
A place where you await execution for crimes committed
Oh but if only to JESUS your life was submitted
The World as we know it today is awaiting execution
For Capital crimes extending from forsaking God, denying Christ JESUS, and that of persecution…
Refusing to tithe and letting His commandments in you, abide
For hidden sins you've tried to hide
And God is yet here and loving us still
Call on Him now and believe me, He will…
Deliver your soul from that of Death Row
And return you to a society whereas you will grow
For now is the acceptable time to live free in the Lord and avoid prosecution
Turn to Christ and let him bless you avoid a day of Execution
Believe me, this world in which we live and have come to know
Lives are certainly on that of Death Row
Amen! 2 Peter 3:10

Just Say No... My Testimony

I, William J. Gray, age 45, Born in Dayton, Ohio, give Honor and glory to God for what He has done in my life and is doing today. He is tearing me down, to build me up, thus making me a new creature in Christ.

My present home is Houston, Texas and prior to coming to TDC I was still worshipping drugs and alcohol. I was slowly dying, denying the true and living God. I faced the hands of Death in a *horrible* way. Being bound with ropes on my hands and feet then beaten unmercifully by two men carrying 357 magnums. I was told that I was going to be killed, and just as the man put the pistol to my head and cocked it with every breath in my body, I screamed the Name of JESUS and at that instant, GOD MOVED.

The other man said, "Wait a minute!" "We need to think this out, after we kill him, how we gonna get him out of here?" The man with the gun replied, I have a blanket and some duct tape in my truck. At this time I was struck again with the gun and I fell to the floor. As I lay there, the men went outside, the door was left wide open. I took this time to call on JESUS, asking Him to not let me die, save me, deliver me. Unknowingly, my hands were free, enabling me to untie my feet, and as if someone had picked me up, I had the strength to run free.

Sisters and Brothers, I'm a living witness, and here to tell you, there is *POWER* in the name of *JESUS*. I thank Him for my life and being alive today. Even through I do some "jacked up stuff," as my wife would say, He still is working on my behalf and don't trip, He's not through. There comes a time in our lives when we have to say no to some things, and look to God to help us be steadfast in that choice. God is helping me now, to just say NO to Drugs and alcohol substances that almost cost me my life.

Just Say No!

If you think it's hard to Just Say No let me tell you a story. Drugs played a major role in my life and cost me my children and my wife. Now this was something that I did not want, and when I wanted to quit, the drugs said, "Don't!" I came to realize that I was demon possessed and had to confess!

I am lost and in a make believe world, where drugs are destroying young boys and girls. Now the time has come for me to take a stand, against this demon that now plagues the land. I speak to you who live this lie, stop for a moment and ask yourself why? And what is there for you to gain, when all you're doing is destroying the brain? I was going through this world to and fro, refusing myself to Just Say No. It's easy, if you're willing; it's your life you're spilling, only you that you are killing.

Drugs and alcohol, a suicidal death, self-inflicting pain that you bring on yourself. Refusing to know that I was slowly dying, as I struggled through each day constantly lying. On a suicide mission with no comprehension. Don't be a fatality that folks hate to mention. Live a full life and let the light in you glow. When it comes to drugs, Just Say No!

Please listen to me and what I have to say, because it will be good for you to have heard some day. You're hearing from a man who is a recovering addict. In and out of prison, "MAN I"VE HAD IT!" I took inventory of my life's story, and found it was drugs I was giving the glory. Opportunities awaited me at the door, but I shook them off because I wanted to score.

There was a time in my life when I could have done well. If I'd Just Said No to those with drugs to sale. The things that I had, they were taken away, "A fool and his money will part one Day." I stole from myself and took from my home. I was at the point of loosing all that I owned. I took the money that I had and invested in drugs, I hung out in the streets with dirty low down thugs.

I played with my life in a drug "parade," not even aware I could have been a victim of AIDS. An I.V. user, a drug abuser...If you don't say NO, you become a loser. If you stay in the mix, drugs will take its toll, so please set your sights on much higher goals. Drugs and alcohol are nothing but a mind trick, a substance that is used only by the SICK. Drugs will have you thinking you are something you're not, and you'll live forever where it's burning hot! Take control of your lives, while you now still can.

SAY NO TO DRUGS A PLAGUE UPON THE LAND! In the name of JESUS. Amen!

Slipping Into Darkness (A Testimony)

When I was young and coming up,
I hung out with those whose lives were corrupt.
I frequent clubs, chased girls, stayed in bars.
I partied, robbed, and stole everything but cars.
My mother at night would hear sirens,
Many nights she'd awake out of sleep with loud screams,
She'd often wondered where I was, or if I were ok,
She's gone now; my dear mother has passed away.
I can still hear her voice ringing in my ear,
"Son, if you don't stop what you're doing, for your life I fear."
However, being young I didn't know better,
So I continued life in the fast lane not knowing whether,
To stop and try to understand or even hear what was being said,
When a deceitful voice spoke, "Don't bother, go right ahead!"
There I was thinking I was having big fun,
Drinking, Smoking, Near death looking down the barrel of a gun.
What would it take for me to get out of the game?
JESUS, my friend, Be Born Again!
I often wondered what it would take to Regain the yester years,
To have found my way out of darkness that had so many drowning in tears,
There were so many people, who cared for me and shared in my pain,
And there were those who'd say my what a pity and a shame.
But friends, Christian friends who care and see you slipping away,
For you, would pray each and everyday,
Praying to God that you would turn from your wicked ways;

And turn to JESUS and give Him Praise.
God knows your condition and that you grieve,
And He will take you out of darkness if you only believe.
Trust in His Word and let Him guide your path,
If you stay in darkness you'll only face His Wrath.
For in this world we live a lie,
Where Satan is a liar,
The Love of JESUS should be our hearts desire.
Slipping into Darkness, the wiles of the devil.
It's nothing to brag about so why do we revel?
King Jesus, Jehovah Jirah, Lord of Lords who has all power!
Power to destroy the prince of darkness who has had his hour.
I share with you in these last days,
Its time we give our lives to Jesus and turn from evil ways.
Don't be left behind when the Rapture Comes,
Turn your life over to Jesus and Join the Holy Ones.
The Lord is calling those of us Lost in Sin,
He wants to Restore in us New Life that will never end.
He's calling, hear the Voice, Hear the Cry for your Salvation.
For it fills His Heart to know there is a separation…
From Darkness to Light, from Wrong to Right.
Amen.

A Soldier's Story

It was early morning August 1993 when the words of a song came to me,
Words that had significant meaning,
Words that were of God that went something like this...
We are soldiers in the Army,
We have to fight although we have to Cry,
We have to hold up the blood stained banner,
We have to hold it up until we die...

These words stayed in my mind,
And with much inspiration, I wanted to become,
For the glory of God, A Soldier.
To be enlisted into the Army of God, the Most Powerful Regiment known to man...
The United States Army of God. These words are of great importance in our lives.
And I will attempt to give to you, for God's glory, "A Soldier's Story."
August 1993 I, William Gray enlisted into the Army of God.
Upon enlistment, I became a born again soldier,
Resurrected from the dead in Sin to a full pledge Soldier,
A private, accepting Jesus Christ as my personal Savior.
Accepting Jesus as my personal Savior meant, having my own personal protection,
As I would soon go into battle against, The Enemy.
August 11, 1993 I went into battle,
Frontline face to face with the enemy,
People whose conversation were not of God,
Cursing, Lust of the Flesh, whoremongers, blasphemers, temptation... Prison.
Upon enlistment I had to endure much training,
I had to be fully aware of who the enemy was and the weapon needed to defend myself in combat.
My training was intensive and began immediately.

I was becoming a good enlistee,
I studied; I worked hard, working diligently to learn combat.
I was given the tools that held the power to win any war...
The Holy Bible, The Word of God.
When used accordingly, and to the will of God,
This, the most powerful weapon known to man,
And inspired of God, Would enable me to stand against the enemy,
August 11, 1993 I was taken by storm,
Attacked from both sides.
Surviving the blows, The fiery darts,
I remembered my protection, my personal savior.
I retreated to my foxhole, my cell, and retrieved the ultimate weapon,
My bible, for further instructions in defense against what would seem to be an ongoing battle,
The Lord spoke to me, and moving on the Spirit.
I began to read Eph. 6:13... Wherefore take unto you the whole armor of God,
That ye may be able to stand in the evil day,
And having done all, to stand.
So, I girted my loins with Truth, I had to strap up,
Putting on the breast plate of Righteousness,
Strapped my feet with the preparation of the Gospel of Peace;
Taking the shield of faith that I may Quench all the fiery darts of the wicked... The Enemy.
Putting on the helmet of salvation and taking the sword of the Spirit,
Which is the Word of God, and praying without cease in supplication.
Fully armed now, I was prepared for the principalities.
I positioned myself steadfast in the Word,
Not to be moved filled with the Spirit of God,
And now as a born again soldier for Christ,
I'm winning the war with faith!
However, as in any war there will be causalities,

Those caught slipping, caught without the Armor of God.
Having their guards down, their minds seared with that of a hot iron,
Allowing Satan to kill, steal, and destroy.
When in battle you must be alert at all times,
Speaking JESUS, thinking Jesus, breathing Jesus, and most of all,
Loving and Living Jesus.
You, too, can be a soldier in God's army,
He's recruiting daily,
Reaching out to the youth, who whether they know it or not are in World War III and losing.
We Saints of God True soldiers must step in as National Guards,
Encouraging, inspiring, and teaching them the way to survival,
In that, I mean salvation.
I thank God today; I thank Him for giving me these words to say.
I thank Him, I praise Him, and I give to Him glory for inspiring me to share with you...
A Soldier's Story.
Amen.

Evil Among You

You wonder why I speak so much,
Of the world No Doubt,
It's simple, as opposed to Jesus Christ,
Its what its all about,
World separation, world salvation,
And, if I'm not mistaken,
The world is God's Creation,
Though some of us have separated from the World,
And many of us are reaching out to the boys and girls,
We must be aware and stay aware, realize someone cares,
Know that Jesus is always there,
My, my, to worship and praise our Lord is no more than
Fair.
Jesus is worthy church, we should settle for Nothing Less,
Be Separated from the World and be blessed,
Be filled with the Holy Ghost,
Feel the Presence of Our Lord, Lord of Host.
There are those of you, who strive for the Kingdom of
God,
And surely you do,
You sometimes Fall Short Because there is
Evil Among U,

Satan Tries to distract you with mind tricks,
But when you call on the name of Jesus, Satan moves,
And Moves Quick,
There will always be something or someone,
To try and hinder your mind,
These are Satan and his workers at work,
Against Jesus at all times,

To Rob you of your Joy and Keep you full of worry,
Unable to acknowledge Jesus, and understand that glori-
ous story,
Where Jesus is the Author and who is reliable,

Who gives you Power to stomp Satan Lower, making it
Justifiable,
For Him to flee, Oh if we'd Just open our hearts to thee,

Yes, there's evil among you rest assure,
But it's up to you as Christians to endure,
To Overcome the hard knocks and stumbling blocks,
Because Satan is at work around the clock.

Praise the Lord and worship Him without cease,
You'll feel His presence, and with Joy and Peace,
You'll go through life being loyal and True,
With the Power of Jesus, Rebuking the Evil Among U,
Amen

Menace to Society (A doomed Breed)

It was August 26, 1993 as I sat before the T.V watching the news, when a very emotional broadcast came across. A father of 12 children, and sole provider of his family, was struck down by a 17-year old youth at gunpoint in an attempted robbery. The man was found dead at his doorstep by his youngest son who awaited his father to come home from work. It was his dad's last day at work before taking his vacation. The son anxiously awaited for his dad and would, periodically, run to and fro to the window looking for his father. It was his last trip to the window, that he witnessed his father being approached by a youth and gunned down; murdered.

My friends, we are unfortunate to have in our midst, a breed of youth that have plagued the world with gangland murders, robberies, rape and the sales of drugs, car jacking, and showing no mercy. Although they have become a menace to society, it is apparent that they are a "doomed breed," as well, as a breed of youth who are totally out of control and without morals.

A people who are under the watchful eye of a God who holds the Power that will bring this corruption to an abrupt end. Youth, 18 and under, being manipulated by the power of Satan, his only weapon to draw as many souls to damnation as possible. Corrupting the minds of children who really don't know what time it is and have not been educated in the ways of righteousness. A "doomed breed," children unaware of the savior, unaware of their purpose in society.

A people who have not been taught the true meaning of life, and who apparently do not know that the wages of sin is death. A breed of people who are "lost" and know not the way, the Truth, nor the Life. It is written, however, that these times would come and come to past. Times when children would rise up against their parents and rebel against authority. But, the Father of

Salvation, The Ruler, The Creator who's color is purity, and who is "The Blood," The Lamb... Jesus Christ.

The one who will bring down the strongholds that plague our society, who will destroy those who are not only a menace to themselves but a "Menace to Society." He is one to whom every knee must bow and every tongue confess that He, Jesus Christ, is Lord. The only True Leader whose gang is a band of Angels. Saints who believe on Him and who worship Him in Song and Praise.

He is our Savior who came that we might be Saved; saved from corruption, destruction, and Menaces to Societies. Those that have chosen not the way of the Master an already "Doomed Breed." Genesis Chapter 6 Verse 11... The Earth also was corrupt before God, and the earth was filled with violence. And God looked upon the Earth, and, Behold, it was corrupt. For all flesh had corrupted his way upon the earth. And God said unto Noah, The End of all Flesh is come before me; For the Earth is filled with violence through them; and, behold, I will destroy them with the earth.

As we know it, God had Noah, the chosen one, to build an Ark, because the earth would end in the way of a Flood. If we are really children of God we are well aware that the Second Coming will be of Flaming Fire, taking vengeance on such a corrupt breed of people. It's time, my friends, to make preparations for His Coming... Are you ready? Don't be caught dead without Jesus. Call Him up now because Saints are standing by to take your call and the number is Toll Fr.ee Jeremiah 33:3... Jesus, Call on Him and He will show you great and Mighty Things!

Amen.

Last Call

Last Call y'all, and I'm not talking about for alcohol! I am speaking in terms of soul salvation, a close relation, reservation, evacuation, an determination to get out of the devil's territory before the wrath of God takes its course. It's our chance now, at this moment to get what it is God has for us, for surely the devil has come unto us. To sift us as wheat. It is in God's plan however, that we should not perish but yet have everlasting life...

But there are some today that feel they have "time" to make short decisions, that change. They feel they have a little more time to do the things they like and that it'll be alright. They feel they have "time" for that last dance, that last romance with the devil, and its then they find themselves caught up in a whirlwind of sin, feeling as though they have "time" to get it right.

God is speaking today, whosoever will... Come out from amongst them, be ye separate, shake the dust from your feet and prepare to meet the bridegroom. He's saying, "This is your last call, your last chance to spend eternal life with me." This is your opportunity to seek my face; this is your chance, your opportunity to retrieve salvation. This could very well be your "Last Call" to repentance.

The Bible tells us in Rev. 22:12, "Behold, I come quickly, and my reward is with me, to give everyone according to his works." It's "time" that we understand that we, were called out for a purpose and a perfect plan. We have to recognize that this gathering of old and young men, women and girls, is a divine calling—a divine intervention in our lives.

It's evident that God has something for us, blessings be to God right now. I'm striving for obedience. I'm lifting up the name of Jesus, warning individuals of His Coming. Informing those who do not know of His Love, and that He has sent out into the World Messengers of the Gospel. Men and women who share the Good News of Christ Jesus, to let you know that not only is there Good News, but bad news as well. The Bad news, judgment is coming; the day of the Lord is in affect.

God is calling out around the world for the lost to be found even though He has been merciful, graceful, forgiving, and patient. He still extends the opportunity for us to come under the umbrella of faith and be protected from the rain... The Rain of Fire. When we continue to frolic with the devil, we are forsaking the Father; neglecting and rejecting, taking Him for granted and believing we have "time." I can hear some say, "Lord, I know you're coming back, but can you just put it off for Just a Little while longer?" You see, Lord, I met this girl, you know, she's not my wife, she's married to someone else, but she promised me some Kool Aid, and Lord, I want it."

Rev. 22:9 tells me... he who is unjust let him be unjust still, he who is filthy, let him be filthy still; And he who is righteous, let him be righteous still; he who is holy, let him be holy still. My Brothers, the Lord is calling us up out of our mess that he may bless, so don't second-guess, Let's progress.

The Lord illustrates daily the seriousness of being saved because in many of our lives the Lord is having mercy; giving us grace and calling us into a Higher place. I stand before you in the name of Jesus, a servant of God, to tell you that it is my belief that we are at the stage of witnessing history repeat itself. (Luke 21:27) This being so, prophecy is therefore being revealed and fulfilled and this tells me, we don't have much, time.

Last Call for the high-minded, the great and the small, these who will witness the rise and fall... The players, portrayers, soothsayers, from bareback Africa, to the Himalayas. It may be your Last Call, so let's get it, let's help each other to stay focused and to keep our eyes on the prize and realize the devil is only a disguise; who sets out to tear down the wise.

Take heed my brothers, for he summons you, through His messengers, His Angels, He Subpoenas you into a Higher Calling. For soon the book it shall be open and you will stand before His majesty wondering, shaking, trembling, you had the chance but you forsook that chance for one Last dance, Just one more dance with the devil and that's all... Let's stand up, my brothers, it could be Our Last Call.
Amen.

It Ain't Safe...To Die!

When I look at the abductions, corruption, destruction, eruptions around me. Everyday current events, I realize that the world is really not a safe place to live. When I hear a minister expound on the subject, "life without Jesus," I again realize that it's of the utmost importance to be filled with the love of God, to worship Him, to praise Him, to never leave home without Him.

You never know when the grim reaper will throw in his sickle, you never know when the enemy will attack, but for those of us who know the enemy's soul purpose, which is to kill, steal, and destroy; you should know it's not safe to die if you don't have Jesus. We go through life happy go lucky, unaware of the evil that lurks around us, not even aware that Satan has an army of demons seeking whom they may devour.

Rivals of the true and living God, who opposes and despise everything Jesus stands for. With this in mind, we should keep God's Word hidden in our hearts. If you think its safe to go through life without Jesus, then you'd better think again. Life is but a vapor and tomorrow is not promised. Don't be caught dead without Jesus, put on the whole armor of God and walk in His Light because the writing's on the wall, and believe me, It Ain't Safe.

Destruction, innocent lives taken at the hands of terrorist, devil worshippers, occults, those who seek revenge against the governments, the Oklahoma bombing, Columbine, Virginia Tech Massacre, Flight 800, Flight 3407, the Tsunami, Paris. It ain't safe.

Corruption, leading the way to sin. The sales of drugs, gangland murders, drivebys, scandals, illicit sex, trafficking and trading... it ain't safe. Eruptions, can you feel the shake, the quakes? Church, it's time to awake, it's time for Jesus. We've got youth rebelling against authority, children rising up against their parents. Wars, famine, fatal disease; AIDS, an epidemic that's taking the lives of many. Carriers of this deadly virus are sometimes unaware they have it and pass it on in a moment of Passion... In the Heat of the Night.

Just when you think everything is normal or going well, the unexpected takes its course. What could happen, likely it will. It's just not safe to go through life uninsured. I'm speaking of having a life long policy with Jesus. We need God's protection at all times because we are living in perilous times and scripture tells us that "If you know these things, see then that you walk circumspectly, not as fools but as wise, redeeming the time, because the days are evil (Eph. 5:15-16)."

The World Trade Center, Paris France, Oklahoma City, Virginia Tech, Ferguson, these were sad occurrences that express a time to wake up because God is trying to get our attention. It's not safe anywhere, anymore, and the more reason why we should be under the Blood Covering of Jesus. This is no plaything we're dealing with in today's society. Sick, twisted, evil hearted, people exist in this world, true workers of iniquity and what goes on in their minds, only God knows.

Therefore, we need to be mindful of the seriousness of being saved. If you should die now, today, where would your soul rest? If you're not sure, and you don't have Jesus, seek Him now while He can be found. Amen.

An Invasion on Earth

It's an eerie feeling probing the night air,
It kind of makes you feel, something is out there,
But what could it be, something you cannot see?
It's hard to figure, it looks like you are me,
It will take on the form of whatever it choose,
People will think you're high, or maybe on booze,
Aliens, extra-terrestrial beings, can believe what you're seeing...
Invasions are something you can start believing

Can you imagine what could be out there in space?
High technology staring you in the face,
It's studying your moves and all your ways,
And there's nothing you can do to even phase,
It's changing daily just to be like you,
It camouflages itself to watch what you do,
It's an uncanny feeling and a mystery at that,
But it's all about invasions, now, to be exact,

Invasions of privacy, body, church, and minds,
Corrupting the ways of mankind,
But what can you do or even say?
Yes, get down on your knees and to Jesus, pray,
Falling stars, UFO's, flying saucers, tell me, who really knows?
"It landed over here, no, it landed over there!"
Rest assure, it will land somewhere

It may seem to you as a mystery
But we'd better get wise or we'll live in misery,

You see, invasion is a word that arrives from somewhere which brings to mind...
Something is out there; it's already here, so please believe,
Don't continue life being deceived,

Blacks, Hispanic, and even Caucasians,
It's something evil, expect an invasion!

Let me put this on your mind, encounters of all kind,
Invasions are existing throughout mankind,
Stop and think about what I say,
We're being invaded each and everyday.
You can talk on the phone; you think you are alone,
Take it from me; you've got it all wrong.
The IRS in all of her finesse...
"How much money have you hid in your nest?"

I'll tell you now how evil it is,
And it gets even worse as we get through the years.
Listen, it would seem to me we're in a race for space.
But what could be out there other than disgrace?
When will we see or even learn?
What's out there in space is not all our concern.
Talk about invasions, we'd best take heed,
Think about the needs and cease with greed.
To start a new life, their hearts do yearn,
But look at the space shuttle and how it burned.
God has a way of making examples
Don't test God; His word you trample,
This is something not meant to be,
This is man's doing; just you wait and see.

Invading God's turf, for what it's worth,
We'd best take heed and find New birth,
Be Born again, right here on earth.
Where we're supposed to be.
Get our hearts right and then come see,
In a shuttle for you that's pre-designed,
To dwell in Heaven that's outlined...
In your Bible, where JESUS is reliable,
Any other means is suicidal.

I'm telling you what I know, not something I heard,

Cease with invasions and obey God's Word!
Space Age a worldly rage,
Let's put our lives in its perspective gauge,
Because all the money you put into space,
You're killing hungry children of the human race.
And those of you who think all is good,
It's because you're dumb and want it not understood,
But, God knows what is your plan,
The works of Satan to destroy the Son of Man.

JESUS Christ, for you paid a price,
These fruitless invasions aren't very nice.
Put this in mind as you journey on,
Remember what I said about the telephone.
Keep worshipping those things you know are not right,
And you live eternally in the night (darkness),
Blind and in space, what a terrible waste,
What will they do when it's God they'll have to face?

We'd better wise up and open our eyes,
We're not alone and what a surprise!
There's a "TRUE INVADER" in whom we all will know,
And soon, very soon, He's going to show!
A close encounter of the worse kind,
An Invasion on Earth...you think I'm lying,
Coming in a formation like you've never seen,
For those who have lived The Word and have kept their hearts and minds clean.
And, as for you who refuse or deny JESUS
Oh well, it's sad to say, but you'll burn in Hell!
Amen

Running Scared. “The Day of the Lord”

An alarm has been sounded in the Holy Mountain; the trumpet blows in that of Zion. The clouds open with a loud noise… And those Standing in the Earth… Lose their Poise. All that live in the Earth, tremble, for the Lord and His army have now assembled. “The Day of the Lord” is now at hand… “Woe unto you”… says The Son of Man. Darkness and gloom now covers the earth, the clouds are thick, as if to burst! From its midst, God’s army does appear… the sinners of the earth, run in fear.

“Running Scared,” for the day has come, the arrival of the King… The Holy One. Along with Him, a people great and strong… Recruits like who has never before been, ordained of Christ to make desolate those still in sin. For never has any army seen one such as this… King Jehovah Jireh is now in our midst. What is like this mighty people we see? Before them a fire—a flame behind… Woe unto thee! The land before them was like the Garden of Eden, but now it’s as if it has been weeding.

Nothing that lives will even escape, “The Day of the Lord…” it’s too late. Warning had come, and now its destruction. The earth and its works… iniquity, and corruption. “Running Scared,” for they’ve witnessed nothing like it. Running, hiding, they can’t even fight it. For they come for you, O’sinner man… With a great noise, leaping mountains, sword in hand. Like the noise of a flaming fire that devours the stubble. A strong people in battle, coming to bust your bubble. All in their way, will squirm in pain… No time now to try and explain.

Faces are drained, the color is gone, people cry out…”What’s going on?” They run like mighty men, climbing trees, over walls, “running scared.” Please hear me, y’all they climb the walls like men of war, everyone marches in formation, and they do not break ranks. They do not push one another, everyone marches in his own column. Though they lunge between the weapons, they are not cut down...

They run to and fro in the city, For there is no pity. They run on the housetop, they climb into houses not thinking, twice they scatter about as little mice, climbing in windows as that of a thief. "The Day of the Lord..." There is no relief! The earth quakes; the heavens tremble, the sun and the moon grow dark. The day of the Lord is upon man, and life has reached its mark.

The stars have given up its brightness, the light has gone away. The people are running scared: because now... it's Judgment Day. The Lord gives Voice to His army, for they are mighty and great, for strong is He who executes His Word... No time to negotiate. "The Day of the Lord" is great and terrible as well... Be among the righteous, my children, for the unrighteous will have failed. Amen

Like Father Like Son (The Curse)

I really never got a chance to know my dad, but rumor had it… he was kind of bad.
At a very young age, for some reason. We had to part, my mother gathered us up for he had broken her heart.
As time went on and I grew up, I thought about dad, I wouldn't give up.
Some how or another I thought things would change, I was wrong, everything remained the same.
So there I was in an all-new land,
In the care now of grandma's hands.
My mother went on to seek a new life;
As time went by…She was no longer a wife.
Life with grandma, Mrs. Myrtle E Mitchell, was an extraordinary one, She loved to pickle pears, apples, fruits of all kind…
I would forget about Dad , in season, in time.
A thought had crossed my mind at a particular time, "Did I want to grow to be like that dad of mine?
Always fussing, abusing, and even hating, all the things, which are considered degrading.
As time went on and the older I got,
My life was veering into something it should not.
I did some things I should not have done,
I was now in the pattern of… Like Father, Like Son.
Being disobedient and neglecting correction I later ended up in the Texas Dept. of Corrections,
It was then I became aware of the facts.
The facts of life, whereby I'd get back on track.
My mother's love and thinking of our welfare, she tried desperately to put a father figure there in our lives and we could see…
One husband, two and then three… I guess it wasn't to be.
My life home, that is, from corrections, I tried to live with that of perfection.
I was honest, trustworthy, and reliable…

It was there I learned much about the Bible.
It was there, prison, I learned the true meaning of like Father Like son.
Through Jesus, the Holy Spirit, The Holy One.
The one and only faithful and true Father in Him no need to worry why even bother.
It is my wish to walk after Him,
No more rock and roll, but spiritual hymns.
Respecting the Father I only know now,
Abiding in Him the best way I know how.
My new Father, whereby on Earth no man should be called Father, the Father who does everything right.
The father in whom I'd like to be like.
The father in whose image I was made,
The Father who, for my sins paid...
The Ultimate Price, the Greatest Sacrifice
Amen

Evil Among You… "Ain't Nobody Listening"

Anytime you purpose in your heart to do what is right, (anything right is of God,) opposition is going to be there. Someone or something will come against you to throw you off track or take you out the game. The devil doesn't want to see you prosper simply because he's been stripped of his prosperity.

The spirit of the Lord is showing me that the devil is rising up against men that want to do what's right. Satan's motive is to bring down the man of righteousness. Saying this I'm reminded of Adam and Eve. The woman allowed the devil to persuade her into eating from the forbidden tree. It is known that men can be so naïve, gullible and easily influenced when it comes to women. Satan used the woman to trigger the trigger, "Ain't Nobody Listening!"

We should know the devil is evil. His soul purpose is to kill, steal, and destroy. In this day and time, you can go to prison for any one of these crimes. Let me be real with you, right now the devil is trying to kill me, he knows I have a medical condition, extreme hypertension, he's attempting to steal my marriage thus "destroying" our home using chaos and confusion. God is not the author of confusion, Satan is and we were not made in his image! Ain't Nobody Listening, you hear me but are you listening? There is a difference.

God is speaking but Ain't Nobody Listening. We hear him speak on Sunday mornings but do we really listen? Do we fake our understanding of what God is saying to whomever in His Word? I'm not pointing any fingers because I'm guilty and I stand accused.

When I mentioned Adam and Eve and how the devil used the woman Eve to influence the man Adam, the scripture comes to mind, where we wrestle not with flesh and blood but principalities in the air, demonic forces in high places. The Bible tells me in Matthew 10:36 "Your foe," "Your enemy" are those of your own household. Satan doesn't care who he uses to initiate chaos and if you are not fully protected, knowledgeable, he will drop a Spirit in you that will have you acting like him. Again, we were made in God's image, not his... I'm saying all this to inform you that there is evil among you.

My Pastor "Anthony Mosley"

My pastor is a mild mannered man. A man of humor, a great teacher and anointed of God to express the beauty of being a Christian. His words are restoring and his purpose... to keep his congregation on track

My pastor has all credentials necessary for the elevation that soon approaches. He is a man that submits to his wife and cares for people's lives, souls. He is a man who stands for truth and is not like other guys. He is a lover of God and not a lover of his self; he is not into worldly wealth.

He is a man who chooses to keep his promises and vows he's made unto God. He is a man who provides for his family and works extremely hard. My pastor is fair, firm, and friendly in exercising discipline. He is a protector, advisor, and a good discerner of men.

He is a man who will admit to his mistakes and knows when he is wrong. Forgiveness to him is a sweet spiritual song. He is faithful to his wife and knows what it takes to avoid strife. One thing is sure, let me tell you, my pastor knows and loves "Jesus." He is a servant of God and not a man pleaser! He is a true man of God and a doer of His work. He's receptive to the Holy Spirit and very alert. He is a man who will stand up for Christ and what is right. I tell you my friends, my Pastor has seen the Light. Amen.

Jesus... A Bridge Over Troubled Waters

In the world today, it is evident that we're living in the midst of troubled times. Disaster is ever present now, and as I speak, somewhere in this world, tragedy is occurring. Some one has found themselves with troubles or a problem that's ruining his or her life. Somewhere a family is coming a part because of a divorce (infidelity and divorce ensues) or unable to meet a bill (about to lose your house). A son or daughter is incarcerated and facing the death penalty, leaving a loving family troubled and weary.

So many of us have crossed over to the other side, however, to find "trouble" and it would seem there is no way back or out. But I'm here to share with you; there is "A Bridge Over Troubled Waters." Looking back over the years of my life, I can see why I'm where I am today. Why so many young people have fallen away from their calling in life and are headed for prison.

If not prison, the ultimate in destruction, which is death. Many of our youth are troubled with rebelling not listening; being of a rebellious nature can be a main factor as to why there is so much violence in the land. Our up bringing, refusing the instruction of our parents or pastor. Being misled by principalities, falling into the many snares Satan has laid out. His purpose is to capture as many souls as he possibly can. Times have changed, however, since my childhood and life seems to move now at a much faster pace.

It seems that the most important thing in life today is having ropes and chains, swinging things. Having things by any means necessary—tricked out cars, the latest in fashion, the bling, anything of material value. To get these things many again find themselves in "trouble." Trying to come up, robbing, stealing, and selling drugs is not the way. These only make way for trouble, which is what Satan is all about. Be mindful however that there is a bridge over troubled waters; that there is a solution to all your troubles... Jesus... He can fix it!

Sometimes I ask myself, "Will there be another generation to come?" Surely not if our troubled youth continue destroying their lives, being disobedient or of a rebellious nature, and not seeking what is pure and wholesome...Jesus is the way, the truth, and the life. God has a calling on each of our lives. He has something better planned for us and I say to our troubled youth, troubled America for that matter, take time out.

Be submissive and receptive to the Holy Spirit. Be obedient and live honest lives. Give yourselves and others the chance to seek God's help and guidance; He gave His son Jesus Christ to be your "Bridge Over Troubled Waters." He shall deliver thee in six troubles: yea, in seven there shall be no evil to touch thee." Job 5:19 Amen.

Psalms

Oh **I Want To See Him**, to look upon his face.
To be in the comfort of His bosom, that **Amazing Grace** for once I lived the life.
In a world that was lost, but now, here I'm found, thanks to **The Old Rugged Cross**.

There was a time in my life, when I was all the way down,
Well, until I received Jesus, now my feet are planted, **On Higher Ground.**
Jesus said to me, son, if you'll turn to me, and repent of your sins,
In your life, I'll **Rise Again**.
I'll over shadow you with **love,** and my spirit I'll give to you
If you'll just worship and praise me,
With psalms of Alleluia.

There will come a day, when there'll be no more wonder,
I'll be caught up with my savior, **Going up Yonder.**
Not only is this trip for me,
You can do the same...
Lift Jesus up, and **Glorify His Name!**
Worship Him, praise Him, and do your alms,
Bless the Lord, with spiritual psalms.
Don't put off for tomorrow, what you can do today...
Now is the time for salvation...
This is the day.
Amen.

Lifestyles

This life I live, it is not my own. It's a life I chose though, as I have grown. I loved to party, have fun and things... To prey on lustful women, and to their bodies cling.

I loved to drink, as it confuses my mind, to a world that is cold, and very unkind. It takes me to a level, where I thought I'd never been, a level that resulted in a life of sin.

My glory was in those finer things in life, gold, silver, diamonds... a 10 for a wife. The best of cars sitting on 20s. My clothes, my jewelry...money a plenty

Rolling out with the elite, sipping and capping, cognac, chardonnay, I thought this was the happenings. Nothing could change, the way I felt... Until one night, on my knees I knelt.

For something happened that would change my life I was at the point, where I was about to lose my wife... My children, my home...everything I owned.

I was tricked by the devil... and was left all alone.

It was the lifestyle I chose which left me in despair. Those I thought were friends, they were no longer there. I realized my style of living was not what God had intended, my lifestyle became a reality... as I had **repented**.

God has now come into my life, and has thus rearranged my thoughts, my behavior, and things just ain't the same. I can see clearly now, for the storms in my life have ceased... There's a newness in me...A wonderful and sweet release.

I party now with **Jesus**... I drink **New Wine**. I'm in fellowship with **a family,** who is Holy and divine. I know longer worship idols, nor prey on seductive women... **God Promised to Blessed Me**... if I would stop my life of sinning.

He promised me in **His Word,** there would be a cleansing. He gave me a gift to write, for souls I'd be winning. The lifestyles of the rich, and that of the famous... Tactics of Satan, my brothers, his means to claim us.

To get us **Caught Up,** in the pleasures of this world. Pleasures that have corrupted, the minds of our boys and girls. The lifestyle we choose, however, can be hazardous to our wellbeing. If we're not in **Christ**, were only deceiving... ourselves, those around us, and people we love... seek ye first the Kingdom... and those things above.

Oh, where would I be had I continued my lifestyle? I thank God for **Jesus**, who was there, all the while. I thank Him for this new life... A new lifestyle... I thank Him for blessing me, His son...his Child.

I thank him for receiving me, back into the fold, for the lifestyle I chose, at one time seemed right... But I've learned that it results in death and **loss of Sight**... **Sight of God** and His will for me... I have a new **lifestyle** in Jesus... for God had mercy on me.
Amen

All praises and glory to God who inspires me to write all things.

Play No Games

Jesus, now being the author of my life, things are not the same.
The **old** has been put away, and now **I play no games.**
I've put off the old man and have been dressed **anew**.
My plans are to enter His gates, what about you?
For many are called but few are chosen,
Playing those worldly games, hearts have frozen. Principalities have taken over the minds of our boys and girls,
no more do I care for the activities of this world.
Jesus, for whom all praises are due,
The forsaken father who plays no games with you.
Priorities are forgotten, minds have become rotten,
And on His Word, His Name...We have trodden.
It's Time Out... **Play No Games.**
Seek ye the Kingdom... Your claim to fame.
Come out from among them and into the marvelous light,
Separate from the world and do what's right.
Stop playing games and thus live for the Lord.
Why do we make something so simple, extremely hard?
This is not the way life was designed to be...
Play No Games... Please, hear me.
God is getting angry, and His wrath daily shows,
Take heed to His Word and learn from them who know.
For God is the Creator and the Ruler of All.
The Alpha and the Omega... The rise and the fall,
The Beginning and the End...
He's saying to us today... **Play No Games,** My Friend.
Amen.

Peace Be Still

There's not a day to go by that certain things seem to come my way. Individuals who profess to know the Lord and yet, prove contradictory at heart. They quote scriptures as if they were preachers, but ask if he or she would like to be disciple or maybe a teacher. The answer you'll get will make you fret, it'll make you wonder, "Do they really know where it's at?"

They appear to be truly in the Lord, but then, after a while, they love Satan hard. Disrupting, condemning, starting up strife, and even hatin'; you can't tell me they don't worship Satan. They know of the lord but harden their hearts. Jesus said, those kind and I are sure to part. I'll tell you what I know and found to be true. Today's heathens or hypocrites, they are never through.

They talk about this. They talk about that. Refusing themselves to accept the fact, that dealing with God is no plaything; For He knows our hearts, minds and everything. Satan can make things look so good to you; he can even make it sound good too. Jesus said, "My will be done," but some of the people you hear, you'd think they're the one. After good talks and righteous sayings, moments later he and Satan are playing.

We all have a purpose in this life, from the baby to the husband, and to the wife. But, before you speak the Gospel or even teach, first you must practice what you preach. God knows your heart and what is done in the dark. Right now, where you sit is a good place to start; to do that which is the Lord's will, and if you really don't know...

...Peace, be Still. Amen.

The Home Boys "No Limit Soldiers"

They come into the home straight from the streets, broken, tired, needing something to eat. There are men who await you with arms outstretched. Men of fire who were once a wretch. They know your feelings; they feel your pain, they know the cure... Holy Ghost Rain.
They embrace you, love you, feed you the Word, they speak of Jesus, and things you've never heard.
They tell you of Jesus and of His Amazing Grace, they tell you with boldness, and face to face.
They take you, place you in a sweet atmosphere; while you sleep, they are always near.
They're at your bedside, they kneel and pray; they pray for your soul that you would be delivered one day.
They are your servants, waiting on you hand and foot; they read to you stories of Jesus from the Good Book.
They tell you of His healing Power if you only believe, open your heart and thus receive.
Men of God, they take care of you, encouragement and prayer... This is what they do.
They give you Jesus and in a fiery way, you can feel the Holy Ghost, all day as they pray.
They nurture you, teach you, building you up. Some stay—some go...still corrupt.
Stay if you will and consume the Real Deal, The Holy Ghost, my brothers will be revealed.
No Limit Soldiers...What they really are, reaching out to you, no matter how far.
There is no limit to what they can do, leaving no room for error, under the command of one Roman Herrera.
A devout man of much stature and grace; a man of wisdom, humor, and not afraid to get in your face.
No Limit Soldiers, Regiments for Christ. Who go out into the world and tell you of the Greatest Sacrifice.
Freddie Garcia had a wonderful idea, taking addicts off

the streets…No Doubt, No Fear.
Restoring their minds, and even their lives; that they may return to society, to their children and their wives.
As for the Home Boys, The Soldiers SW 38, keep hope alive, for with you, it's never too late.
For God is inspired with your Holy Ghost Fire, and I believe with all my heart, Home Boys, you're His hearts desire. Amen.

Where Would I Be

As I look at my life, the lifestyle I chose, I began to realize how dangerously I was living. I realize it now because God was there and had mercy on me...A Sinner.

When I found myself outside the will of God, I was actually playing Russian Roulette with my life. I was daring, defying, and simply denying God. I was a macho man, a Mandingo warrior. I was a fool who did not understand. I did not understand that this way that seemed right for me, was actually a set up by Satan to destroy me. The results of my taking this avenue in life would eventually lead to death, had I not had a spiritual awakening.

From my understanding of God's Word, I find that this death is but bodily, but the soul lives eternally, in hell or heaven. In hell where there will be wailing and gnashing of teeth. In heaven where there will be no more crying as we walk the golden streets. A city of gold and gates of pearl, the New Jerusalem, a totally different world (rev. 21:22-27)

Where would I be had it not been for Jesus loving me? Where would I be had I continued with this lifestyle of the un-free? Where would I be? I've looked down the barrel of death, I've felt the sting of death as I injected the venom into my arm. Illicit sex with women who could have done my body harm. I was drinking, drugging, humbugging, hanging out with the young and the restless, who will forever be thugging..."Where Would I be?"

Robbing from myself, stealing from my wife, fussing, lighting, stabbed with a knife. Emergency room trauma, a life of drama, refusing to listen to a spirit filled mama. Rebellion, a hellion in every since of the word. Where would I be if I had not received the Word? It was Jesus who intervened in my life, it was He who sat me down and showed me how I was treading dangerous ground.

He showed me love and told me in His Word, He wishes not that I should Perish...His goodness and mercy I shall always cherish. He speaks to me daily in that small, still voice. Do you want him or do you want me, it's really your choice? Just remember, I was there for you when you cried out in pain, once again, your life was sustained. You stumbled, you fell, your life was pitch black. Your wife put you out and refused to take you back. Your life was in doubt and family counted you out.

You were as Israel to me...I brought you out! I restored you in mind, in body, and in health. I was there for you after you tried everything else. Where would you be my friends had it not been for Jesus? Idolaters, fornicators, men pleasers, God is here and He has your back. He has you covered when you become under attack. I don't know about you, but let me tell you about me. I'll be living for Jesus for without Him, where would I be? Amen.

The Enemy (Prelude)

Over the past week we held a marriage seminar. We had a women's conference and we touched on sensitive subjects within our homes. We were given distinct instructions as to what to do to alleviate any on going problems. But, the puzzling thing about the whole ordeal, Satan was ever present and very disturbed. He was angry because the Word was going forth; the truth was being told, a remedy was about to unfold, and marriages were about to be complete.

Love was about to resume, however, this was not the way Satan would have it to be. So, therefore, he dispatched his military force against the church, attacking the members, trying to discourage marriage. He tried to discourage members from coming to church. Attacking the prayer warriors, the mothers of the church, and the usher. He created chaos in the church.

Fights among our youth on church grounds, a movement in the church was causing distractions as the Word was going forth. It's evident that the devil has been loosed; going about like a roaring lion seeking whom he may devour...woe unto you! He means us no good and truly he is **"The Enemy"**... I would say its hammer time, its time to put Satan in his place. Ambassadors in Christ I give you The Enemy.

The Enemy

Who is he that cometh but to kill, steal, and destroy? Who is he that setteth before you temptations—decoys, snares to entrap you, to keep you from being free? "Who is he?" Why, if you do not know, he's the enemy!

He's the one, whom, if you will let, will rob you of salvation. He will hinder you from pressing on, and make void your preparations, for the kingdom of the Lord and life eternal, to that of the pits of hell... A Flaming inferno.

He is your adversary, and he has no love for you. He is the father of hate, and there's no telling what he will do. He lies in wait to attack your mind, and he will enter in if you get laxed in **the Wor**d and give him time.

He will attempt to **kill** the spirit, that spirit of joy; he will **steal** your soul, and trust me, he will **destroy**, everything of righteousness if you allow it to be. There's no doubt in my mind... he's the enemy.

He has the world in a state of illusion; Satan, the enemy, the author of confusion. Attacking our youth leaving them in a rebellious state, instilling in their minds to destroy and hate.

We're at war Christians with principalities of the air, put on the whole armor of God and enforce our rights; be spiritually strong and armed with **The Word**, when confronted by the **Prince of Night.**

Be mindful church, anything of good he comes against, and if you stop to think, nothing he does makes any sense. Filling the world with gadgets and tricks, luring you further away from God's word is about it.

Testing your ability to stay strong in the Lord, awaiting the opportunity to catch you off guard. To get you out of church and away from the spiritual guide, back into the world, where you only backslide.

Slipping farther and farther into that of the dark, reaching, grabbing, but can't seem to find the mark. Falling from God's grace and loving kindness, into the hands of **The Enemy** into eternal blindness.

I'm here today to warn you of what's going down'. **Satan, The Enemy,** is in your town. What defense have you set up to ward off his attack?"

Be filled with "**The Holy Ghost**..." He Can't touch that! Amen.

Move...Get Out the Way

Why is it so hard for us to let God work in our lives? Why is it we get caught up in situations and find ourselves unable to get out of them? We struggle and strain and still nothing seems to change. We hold on to past hurts, we harbor animosity; we will not let go and let God have His way, where situations in our lives are concerned.

We some times become **judge, advocate,** and **jury**. We've tried **all** and nothing seems to get us where we need to be. We want desperately for whatever situation we've encountered to just disappear to the point where we try to do the impossible ourselves, but God is saying... "**Move, Get Out the Way!**" Let me handle the situation, the battle is not yours. I am who I am, the author and finisher of your faith. Who knows better what you're going through than **Jesus Christ!** Move... Get Out The Way!

We've been in situations far worse and Jesus was there for us. Sometimes we find ourselves being provoked to anger when we should be humble. We set out to fix the situation on our own and find ourselves all messed up, even worse than before. There are times when we don't understand what's really happening and at this time we should look to Jesus for assistance and strenght. The Bible says, "Lean not on your own understanding." Our understanding of things is sometimes abstract and where there is no understanding, there is confusion, and confusion is of the devil.

Believe me, we need, in this day and time, to rely more on **Jesus** and get out of self and look to the hills from which comes our help. Let go of the things that easily beset us. Let go of that which is above your capacity, and let God fix it. God is saying in so many words, **"Move, Get Out of the Way!"**

We've messed up time and time again, but we wont let go, we wont stand, instead, we want to do it ourselves; and it's self that get us in the mess we're in today. Move my friends Get out of God's way; let Him rule in your life and Fight your battles. Let Him mend broken hearts, restore marriages, and resolve all disputes. Give it to God and get out of the way, and see the Salvation of the Lord. Amen.

Goodbye Satan "The Letter"

Dear Satan,

I know you are furious because you have not heard from me, or seen me at any of your establishments. It's one reason why I'm writing you this letter, you see, I'm tired of the way you've treated me. I feel lowly of myself because I was used by you, abused by you, and despised because of you. It's because of you my family left me, my children hated me, friends wanted nothing to do with me.

You made me believe I could have the world, but you only deceived me with your wicked promises. In all actuality you wanted to kill me, to steal my soul; to destroy my life, in which you almost succeeded. But because of my new Friend, I have been saved of your wicked deeds and the plans you had for me.

You told me I had to ride or die, and I believed that lie, but now, I can testify... against you. You thought I would live with you forever. You thought you were cute and clever and I would never leave.

Well, I have made a choice in my life and its to no longer follow you but to now follow Jesus. He has more to offer me and I know He loves Me. He has proven it in so many ways, He laid down His life for me that I may have life eternally. I came to realize hanging out with you, I was spiritually dead, and headed for eternal death.

When I was in your company I found myself miserable, depressed, having no love for others, not even myself; you kept me confused and in doubt. Now, with Jesus, I know what it's all about. With Jesus it's about salvation and with you, its damnation. So I'm writing you to let you know, I don't want you no more I'm tired of your lies, and the way you had me living. So, goodbye Satan.

Sincerely,
William

Goodbye, Old Man

It was March 19, 2007 when I loaded transit bus for downtown San Antonio in route to the Nolan Street Clinic for a scheduled appointment. I was accompanied by 2 of my Home Boys from the victory home, who also had appointments. As we seated ourselves, we began to share "the love of Jesus," when the bus driver yelled, "Hey, keep Jesus to yourself." We all looked at one another with astonishment, and then, silence filled the air.

This encounter took me back to the days of old. I thought about Paul and how he was stoned, beaten; kicked, spit on and talked about because he preached **Jesus**. How can people be so cruel and naïve to not recognize "life;" and how can one be so dumb to come up against the creator, unless..., they just don't know Him.

To reject Christ is to reject life, to reject life is to accept eternal death, a life of torment and a life in Hell. God so loved us that He gave His only begotten Son that we may have eternal life. To reject a God that is merciful and gracious is a sign of one who is "Lost" and have no direction.

Surely this grieves God to know His Son is rejected by a blind world, a world that is caught up with the many devices of Satan. They are a people who have found it more comfortable to wallow in sin, and who have refuse to come out of their comfort zones. These people choose to hang on to that sinful nature, and refuse to say goodbye to the Old Man.

However, "One Day" God will shut the door on all dis-believers, he has every right. He has displayed unconditional love, he has granted mercy, given us grace, shown his love and we say..."Keep Jesus to Yourself, I don't want Him."

Say no to Christ, you say no to life, it is as simple as day and night. In the day there is light, in the light there is revelation, there is Beauty...Revealed and gives life. Night brings darkness and darkness, to me, brings sleep. A laying down of the body... Death. For the Bible says we must work while it is day, for when night comes no man can work.

God is calling for repentance, either you will or you won't. I would suggest you don't force His hand, for His wrath will come upon the land for when the sky splits and the trumpet sounds, most of you will return to the ground...Eternal death.

Let the Truth be Told, Not Sold

IT doesn't matter if you're young or old,
There's a story to life, let the truth be told and not sold.
If you think it's clever the things you do,
Then lend me your ears; I've got a message for you.

IT'S all about life free of drugs; keeping your life
Clean and free of thugs, disease, plagues handed down as a curse,
To those who deny Jesus' love, you can expect worst.
Before I go any further, let me say some things about the world,
What it can do, the hurt it can bring.

YOU can work all your life and build up treasures,
And simple forget those unexpected measures.
The fancy cars,
All the burglar bars, people will think you are some kind of movie star.
Stylish homes, smart phones, and what will you do when all that's gone?

YOU don't have to be old or young to see,
Time is winding down for both, you and me.
The world is in a rage...role models are carrying aids,
There's a story to life, for you, at any age.
Without "Jesus" in your life, you belong to the world,
Today, the world is like a circus, amusing men, women, boys, and girls,

IT'S time to take an in-depth look into our life story,
Its time to separate from the world and give God His glory,
Its time for the young to think of salvation, its time to make way for a new generation.

CHRISTIANS we must come together and form a bond,
Because there's a job today that needs to be done.
The world is out there on its deepest end, dead-lost, need of a friend.
This is where you and I must play a part, speaking to
The world straight from the heart... on love and peace,
And how it should be, striving for the world to take a closer walk with Thee.

WE'VE got kids walking the streets confused and in doubt,
Not knowing that death and destruction is waiting to take them out.
They're in a world of corruption where there's nothing
But destruction, its like an active volcano, on the verge of eruption.

THERE'S a terror in the day, there's a terror in the night, its time for Christian's to
Display "God's Light," The world is on its last toe—hold,
There's a story about "**JESUS**" that needs **TO BE TOLD... NOT SOLD**.

It's Time

It's time now that we begin to give, give to the Lord who allows us to live. Its time we give to Him respect, your hearts, your minds, your lives, to give Him His due. If you will not, then you choose not to be among "the few." It's time for repentance; its time for convictions in Spirit.

Its time for salvation, its time we lay down our sordid lives and recognize that it's leading us into eternal damnation. Its time we put away those things that easily besets us and hinders our walk. Its time we bridle our tongues and change the way we talk. Its time we realize we've been living a joke, "the earth will melt away, the works therein will go up in smoke" (2 Peter 3:10).

Its time to now seek a better place; stop taking for granted God's mercy and grace. Its time we take a good look around us, seeing what's going on in the earth, and understand what it means to have New Birth. Its time we realize we were born into sin, and that its time we open our eyes and know this life is about to end.

Its time now we prepare to see the king, to go before His majesty for the verdict He will bring. It's time we put away anything unpleasing to God and thus refrain. Its time we humble ourselves and be born again. Its time we realize terror is in effect, destroyers are sent out on a mission and the unrighteous are the elect.

For in Jeremiah 22:6-9 it tells me, and God said it..."I will prepare destroyers against you and your weapon." Please, keep in mind my friends, 2001 Sept Eleven. Its time we now must call on the Lord, pray without cease and not be caught off guard.

Open your Bibles to 2 Tim. 3:1-5 and you tell me if its not time? Its time we make preparations, now more than ever before, the time is near...Even at the door. Amen.

Coming Out of Tradition

Tradition: An unwritten practice passed through generations.

Church is it tradition that every year around the 25th of December, we tell our children, "If you don't be good, Santa's not going to bring you anything for Christmas?" If this is tradition, is it acceptable unto the Lord? I think not for it is surely misleading and truly a deception and an abomination unto the Lord.

It would seem to me that some of us have forsaken our God, simply because we focus more on Santa Claus than JESUS. I Thought Christmas was in remembrance of the Savior, but no more can I tell, according to worldly behavior. The hustle and bustle of the cities, preparing to make a profit, denying the Savior, Christ JESUS the True and Living Prophet.

I know I'm going to step on some toes, but the blood will be on my hands if I don't tell you how the story really goes. Is Kris Kringle, whoever he might be, more important than JESUS? Does he have more power than JESUS? Can he save your soul? "I don't think so!"

Some might say, "Oh, but God doesn't mind, it's just tradition." God does mind if you get caught up in perdition... (Spiritual Ruin). God is a jealous God and is soon to prove it, the wickedness in the earth, He's about to remove it. Please don't be angry with me, I'm only passing on what the Holy Spirit has given me.

Believe me, God is just about fed up with what the world is feeding, things that are practiced not written and are very misleading. I'm not just focusing on Santa, there are a lot of traditions, but what we need to do is prepare for a Special Edition. Acknowledging Christ, the Greatest Gift, the Ultimate Sacrifice.

Santa Claus, we'd best pause and start focusing

on the true and living cause. Tradition: Unwritten practices. We should be practicing on making preparations to see the King, instead of passing on to generations how to make the cash register ring.

It's sad to see so many kids give glory and praise to a man in a red suit. Believe me, deception is not at all cute. Forgive them Lord; for it is not their fault, it's the way they were brought up; the way they were taught. I know this may hit the surface hard, but when we let our kids idolize Santa instead of God, that says a lot.

Each year we create more anger with God, simply because more attention is focused on a man called Santa Clause rather than the Savior called JESUS The Christ. The world is truly in a delusion, and soon, very soon it will be relieved of the confusion. "Blessed is he who is in me, than he who is in the world." I extend this message to every man, woman, boy and girl. We've practiced these traditions long enough. It's time we start coming out of tradition before things began to get rough…Jeremiah 2:7, 9

"And I brought you into a plentiful country, to eat the fruit thereof and the goodness thereof; but when ye entered, ye defiled my land, and made my heritage an abomination. The priests said not where is the Lord? And they that handle the law knew me not: the pastors also transgressed against me, and the prophets prophesied by Baal and walked after things that do not profit. Wherefore I will yet plead with you, saith the Lord, and with your children's children will I plead…"

The Lord God is using me right now, pleading, begging for us to wake up and be ye transformed. He's asking us not to be a part of deception, and to stop misleading our children. Santa Claus has not put one gift in your life, but JESUS has given you the gift of life.

I believe it's time for submission; it's time we come out of some of these traditions. If we keep on with traditions, unwritten practices passed on through generations, we'll find where it is written, we're setting ourselves up for damnation.

Remember church, Jesus is the reason for the season, anything else is treason. Amen.

Do You Remember...

My Sisters, brothers, and fellow Americans it is on my heart to say that we are focusing too much on the World Trade Center and those that lost their lives Sept. 11, 2001. It is in my heart to also say that we truly have our priorities out of context. We celebrate Sept. 11, we uphold the flag to honor those who lost their lives on Sept. 11. We take prayer out of school and yet we establish this day... as a Day to Remember.

We, today, keep in remembrance things that profit not, we honor and keep in remembrance those who God has called home... the inevitable. We're focusing on the wrong thing and its grieving God to the utmost that He's at the point of "Must Return." Sometimes I feel God saying, these people have got me bent. "They must think I'm not, or I want do it. "

We're looking at a nation that can't seem to understand what's actually going on in the earth. Creating havoc over the loss of the Trade Center, the world's choice cedars, not even aware that 76,000 people were destroyed by God because of something David foolishly had done. He took a census and God didn't tell him to. Do you remember? Do you remember when God destroy everyone on earth but 8 people, Noah and his house the reason you are here today... Do you remember?

Do you remember when Jesus died on the cross for your sins and mine that you could have life more abundantly? Do you remember? Do you remember that He got up on the 3rd day with all glory? Do you remember that God gave life a second chance to repent and do His will when He established a new covenant with man? Do you remember Him saying He has the keys, to the gates of Hell? Do you remember Jesus saying, I will return with vengeance and in power? Do you remember the dead will rise first, and then the living to be caught up with Him in glory? Do you remember?

My sisters and brothers in Christ, it is time that we pray for a dying nation, a nation that is dealing with a memory lapse. A nation that remembers everything they want to remember but refuse to remember what thus says the Lord. Do you remember? God said I will punish the wicked and I will destroy the unrighteous... Do you remember Jesus?

At the bottom of the World Trade Center, Ground zero was found amongst all the ruble Beams of all sizes shaped from the destruction in that of The Cross. To put the world, this nation in remembrance of the Savior our Hero...Tell me, do you remember?

Today being Sept. 11, 2002 the world remembers those that were killed in this horrifying event. Today that took place Sept 11, 2001 Americans honor those that gave their lives to save others...today, America Remembers. God gave us the communion that is what we must do in remembrance of Him. Amen

My Daughter

She is special and as sweet as can be. My daughter is "**Precious**," and means the world to me. My daughter is "**Love**"...you can see it on her face... that brilliant glow... you know it's of God's Grace.

My Daughter, she is gifted and in every aspect, having her as my child... Not once do I regret. The things she can do, never ceases to amaze; my daughter has been respectful throughout her blessed days.

She was excellent in School. She knew "**The Golden Rule,**" She knew that **Education** was "**The Fundamental Tool**." The tool for her Success... and her wellbeing... in her, not once, have I stopped believing.

I Love My Daughter; and for many many reasons. She is well trained, well mannered, and thoroughly seasoned. I love my daughter, for she is as beautiful as can be... "**Precious Lil Thing"**... She looks Just like, her **Mother** and **Me.**

In Memory of Michelle Y. Gray... "She Will Be Missed"

Sometimes we're up, sometimes we're down, Sometimes we smile, sometimes we frown.

Sometimes there's joy, and then there's sorrow, for there will come a time when there is no tomorrow.

Michelle Gray a mother, a wife, a sister, and a friend to many of you, and now we must give her, her due.

She was well loved and gave from her heart, the love God instilled in her will never Part.

We will all miss her, that glow, that smile upon her face, but God has informed me that Miki is in a better place. Although we can't undo what has already been done, she would want you all to carry on, in the name of **JESUS**, the only Begotten Son.

For He gave His life, and it is written, we are all appointed a time so don't feel Bitten.

Death's sting cannot take its toll, so keep looking to **JESUS** and He will bless your Soul.

So don't weep, don't moan; don't play a sad song, but yet, Rejoice in the Lord for Michelle Gray is only gone home. She will always be with us and we do know this, but I say unto you this day... "She Will Be Missed." Amen

Facing T.D.C Texas Department of Corrections

Son, when you're robbing and stealing, going the wrong direction, they send you to the Texas Dept. of Corrections. You see, its men down there, they ride them hosse's, you can't call them men because you've got to call them bosses. They tell you what to do, both day and night, and you don't talk back, you say, "Yeah, you're right!" If you try to escape, you may get shot in the head, and then your Mother gets a phone call, "Your son is dead."

All because you chose to live a life of crime in the streets, hustlin', pimpin', beating everyone you meet. The police will stop you and tell you, "You're a cheat!" You think that what you're doing is discreet." Then they take you off to jail, they post no-bail because they want you, my son, your butt they've nailed. Now you're sitting in jail and all you can see is "white," blue and grey "the Colors of T.D.C."

Son, T.D.C is not the place to be, in T.D.C you'll miss your family. So face your goals and your life will be free, because you don't belong in T.D.C.

Now picture this, you're sitting in jail, got to deal with the smell you get to thinking you're under some kind of spell. You've got court in the morning, your stomach starts churning, you think maybe the Judge, he'll give you a warning. Your mind tells you to just wait and see, but your feet tell you, you'll be here in T.D.C.

There you are, sitting in the holding tank, can't even think, too much noise, you've got to bear with the stink. Hours go by and your head is burning, and you say to yourself, "Man, I am Learning!"

I was living the life on skid row, but now I've faced with the turn-row, where the sun beams hot. Dry your eyes, son and wipe the snot.

You sit there in wonder, Am I going under, my

whole life now is one big blunder. You hear the keys jangle, your life becomes tangled, you say to yourself, "There's got to be an angle!" The door opens, and the guard stands, "Court 339! Hold out your hands!" And now, its on with the cuffs, it really gets rough, but deep inside you try to be tough. Standing before the judge you try not to budge, you've been sentenced and now you hold a grudge.

You didn't have the money to hire you a lawyer, and now you feel like a real Tom Sawyer. You had to cop a plea, and now you see. T. D. C is not the place to be. In T. D. C you'll miss your family, so son face your goals and your life will be "free," you don't belong in T. D. C.

The Last Harvest

There's a time to sow, and there's a time to **reap**, there's a time to separate, and there's a time to meet. There's a time to laugh and there's a time to cry, there's a time when the heavens will open, the sky will split, the trumpet will sound, **And People**, **Will Sigh**!

I can remember my childhood days, when I wanted a garden. I always loved the idea of fruit and vegetables coming up from the earth. I was always in wonder about that, amazed even. To take a seed and place it into cultivated ground, in good soil and then in a matter of days, I'm looking at results.

With tender loving care, proper nourishment, I began to treat my plants; watering, insect treatment, keeping them from danger, protecting them from harmful weather. All this care would in time, bring about a **good crop**, a crop that would be Harvest in due season.

In my olden days, I look at how things have changed. How people still plant and grow things, nurturing them to their fullness. But, the quality, the texture, the nourishing content is not as whole as before. Why? Well, due to neglect, abuse, soil erosion, toxic waste and chemicals. Chemicals that induce fast reproductions, chemicals that affect some peoples lives with cancer causing side affects. What has happened to naturalism and the good and wholesome way of **Growth**?

So it is today with man, we are like seeds planted. The Lord took us from the earth, the soil, and formed us into a living, producing being, made in His Image. He nurtured us, gave us strength, wisdom, knowledge, and the sense to know the difference between right and wrong. And all this was good. He breathed life into us that we may have eternal life, following proper instructions and guidance.

We as Christians should be like the plant, the tree

planted by the waters, and that is, not to be moved, corrupted, or unchanged. To be free of pests who will come to destroy you. Who will hinder **your** growth in that of the Lord, and His Righteousness.

If we would just hold fast to what we have, holding on to God's unchanging Hands, His Love, we could grow into a beautiful creation, bearing the best of fruits. Therefore ripen for the Harvest of the Lord, our God.

Yes, Dear People, there will be a harvest. There was a song out back in the day called *Harvest For The World*, the Isley Brothers. You can believe there will be another Harvest, a Harvest for the Kingdom of God --- **The Last Harvest**!

Those found without spot, blemish, and blameless are sure to be harvested. The dead in Christ, those living in Christ, and them that live out His commandments. The day of the crop picker will come, to pluck the good fruit from the bad fruit, the good people from the bad people.

Revelation 22:12 says, "And, behold, I come quickly; and my reward is with me, to give **every** man according as his work shall be."

A Time To Fear

As my pastor would say, "For a thought!" Now, picture this: a mild mannered kid who bothers no one, a honor student who wears glasses; admired by all in his classes. The school bell rings ending another day. The bully, a huge burly kid with a rough, scratchy voice, continually walking, stalking, victimizing his prey. A daily routine as he picks and tortures **the youth**. Ladies and gentlemen, what I'm about to share with you is nothing but the truth.

Now the day came when this humble lad took all he could take, he stood up to the bully, and everyone saw it was a piece of cake. The bully, roaring like a lion, had everyone afraid to speak, preying on those who were humble and meek; but Glory to God, blessed are **the meek**, for they shall inherit the earth blessed are they found in the **New Birth**.

As we see it today, the bullies of the world and the devil is in full steam, truly having his way, or so it seems. But it is written, and again I tell you, the Lord will allow these things to occur but only for a while though. Do let me refer – you and everyone to the book of Matthew, Chapter 24, the Lord speaks of His coming, and the devil deceiving you.

We can preach and teach the love of God and things of good, but if you're not in Christ there's something you haven't quite understood.

In the **Old Testament** the Lord illustrated His being, His power, His **Love** and, **His Wrath.** Now, we find ourselves in the **New Testament**, still in His path. I'm not going to continue to tell you God loves you, instead, I'm going to tell you, **The time is Near** and with boldness and in authority, as God so gives it to me, I tell you Church, **It's Time to Fear**

I'm not trying to frighten you, Please don't think that way. I'm only expressing to you what the Bible says.

If we don't stand up to the bully, that is, **Resisting the devil,** as God is my witness, you'll end up in **The Lake of Fire**, that lower level

Surely the Lord is one of longsuffering and patience, who have endured the test of time; but do you know that patience has its limits? "**We're Running out of Time!**" If your heart is not right, if you've got skeletons in the closet, ungodly deeds you're holding on to, then you don't fear God and you don't believe what He's going to do.

If you think you've got Plenty of Time to get your act together, then really, you should know better. If you're not in **Christ** then its **Time to Fear**, No man knows the day or Hour, but believe me, it's here—near, even at the door. **A Time to Fear**, need I say anymore?

The Book of Matthew, the 24th Chapter however must be preached because There still maybe time for others to be reached.

Chapter 24 verse 14, "**And this Gospel of the Kingdom shall be preached** in all the world for a witness unto all nations, and then shall the end come..."

This is A Time to Fear Church. Already false prophets are here. They have come who claim to be Christ, A time to Fear wars and rumors of wars. A time to fear nations rising against nations and A time to fear kingdom against kingdom. A time to fear Famine, Pestilence, Earthquakes, we can keep pretending, but it's a time to fear.

Dearly beloved we're at t he beginning of sorrows fear ye The Lord, For there could be no tomorrow.

I say to you, The Bible is full of love, mysteries, and compassion, there's also anger, wrath, and destruction if you really love God, it's only your soul He's asking.

In the Name of Jesus Amen.

Pray, Without Ceasing

My friends, I come to you with thanksgiving, sharing my thoughts, and caring about how you're living. As **God** so inspires me to write these things, moreover should we stay in His will, and display good tidings.

We should keep His commandments and walk the righteous path, therefore avoiding the Lake of Fire, that fiery bath.
Praying continually, that is, without cease,
Praying that the Holy Ghost, in you, will increase.

Giving you the protection that you so well need,
To stand against the devil and His evil deeds.
Increasing the power that is everlasting,
Continually praying without a day passing.

Praying to the Father, as He sits on His Holy Throne,
In the Name of Jesus, we make our request known.
All these things to you are a gift,
As we prevail in prayer; Holy hands we lift,

Acknowledging our Lord for all He has done,
Praying without cease until the day He comes—
That is, to take us home to that Heavenly City,
Where there's no more crying; no more pity,
But Joy ever after, peace tranquility,
The Glory of God, from here to eternity.

It is important to us to always pray,
Because we do not know the hour or day
When the Lord will come to retrieve His church,
Thus into our Hearts, will **The Master** Search.

Remove those things that will hinder you from your

goals,
That is, the kingdom of God and saved souls,
Because Just when you think everything's alright,
Sudden destruction – **A Thief in the Night**—
Overcoming you and no way of escape,
The Prince of Light – **Too Late**!

When in constant prayer, a network is set up between you and God, a close contact,
A force field, so to speak , to restrain Satan's never ending attack.
So to combat problems that are ever increasing,
Pray, sisters and brothers, **Without Ceasing.**

A Safe Place... in Jesus

As I take an in-depth look around me, and the occurrences that are taking place in the earth, I become more and more aware of how important it is to be in a Safe environment... **A Safe Place.** For the world today is truly not a safe place to live.

As I look deeply into the activities of the world, it quickens me to **understand**...understand **The Bible**, and that **God is Speaking** as He spoke in the Day of Noah. God is diligently trying to get the attention of those He loves.

Many including myself, have come to the knowledge that **it's time** we seek refuge, shelter from all the storms that now place the earth. Today, violence, crime, terrorism, war, and so much pain and suffering, have become unbelievingly in excess.

Its not safe to walk the streets for fear of driveby shootings, the food we eat because of diseases, and the additives that have become to be known as cancerous. In the workplace, you have the discomfort of wondering whose going to snap, go off because of being fired. The disgruntle worker, we can call him.

Drugs are on every corner, destroying our kids and life in general. Terrorism has become the Big Story today, taking the world by storm, seemingly. There is no defense, no solution, no trust in man's ability to protect his country, and the people who live in it. Suicide bombers, hijackers...it's just not Safe anywhere, anymore.

The churches are under attack, bombings, burning of

churches, the prisons…The priest under fire for accusations against them. The schools, the highways, the byways… **Our Ways**…they are before God. From the beginning of time, man let wickedness enter into the earth and it grieved God that He had made man. And, unless they repent of their sins, He promised to destroy us all. Gen 6:11-13 for reference.

I just look at all the calamity taking place today and I know, **its time** to get it right. It doesn't take a rocket scientist to know, something is going on in our world. With all the disasters, destruction, lives being taken without moments notice. It makes one come to reality, well, he who has a sound mind and fears the Lord. It makes one think… Will I be ready when the Lord comes a calling? Will my house be in order? Will I be in good standing when Christ comes?

To be saved right now, at this very moment, is a blessed assurance that your soul would be in **A Safe Place**. For to be without **Jesus** at a time like this, is ludicrous. **If** you die today, where O where would your soul lie in wait? Would it be Heaven, or would it be Hades? If you don't know, then be assured; accept **Jesus Christ** as your Lord and Savior, your source of refuge your protector, your ticket to Heaven… **A Safe Place.**

To be under the care of **Jesus**, to be in **The Hands** of **God The Almighty** is **The Safest Place** I know; because, today, my friends, the devil is seeking anybody who is without **Christ. I** pray the lost would come to know **Jesus**. I pray those who have hardened hearts, would let go and let God. I pray that this country would seek God's face… My prayer is that we all be found in **The Kingdom of Jesus…. A Safe Place.**

Amen. Giving honor, reverence, and glory to God who inspires me to write these things.

Don't Be Stupid!

1 Peter 1:35 Blessed be the God and Father of our Lord Jesus Christ, which according to His abundant mercy hath begotten us again unto a lively hope By the resurrection of Jesus Christ from the dead, To an inheritance incorruptible, and undefiled, and that fadeth not away, reserved in Heaven for you, who are kept by the Power of God through faith unto salvation ready to be revealed in **The Last Time**.

Sometimes the question comes to me over and over again. What is The Second Coming? The Last Harvest? The Last days? The End? Why does the Holy Spirit reveal this to me? It's simple, its beneficial, and its something He wants **me** to see. I've come to understand, and now I'm more receptive, when the Holy Spirit speaks. I began to put things in its perspective by No means does the Lord want us to be Stupid, But yet, doers of the word. When the Holy Spirit tells you to do something, "**Do it**!"

Right now, the Spirit wants me to share with you **Ignorance is bliss**. In this I mean, there's people out there who don't believe God is going to keep His **promise**. I can hear people saying, "It's not going to happen; it will never be."

Don't be Stupid! These are the very same people who will be around to **See**, believe me!

When we, The saved in Christ, are caught up in the Rapture, Those of ignorance will be left wallowing in their manure, and that's for sure. Excuse Me, but its true though, because they will witness something **they** thought would never be. His Coming, The Great I am, In All Power and Glory, His Majesty.

And its not going to be a pretty sight, and this is why I stress, "Church, Let's keep our Hearts right." Don't be Stupid like so many are. We know the way to Glory, and it's not far. II Peter 3:3-6 "Knowing this first that there shall come in the Last Days scoffers, walking after their own lusts, And saying, where is the promise of His coming? For since the fathers fell asleep, all things continue as they were from the beginning of Creation. For this they willingly are ignorant (stupid), that by the Word of God the heavens were of old, and the earth standing out of the water and in the water. Whereby the world that then was, being overflowed with water, **perished**."

How can people be so stupid? To not believe in the Second Coming? The way things are going in this day in time, I truly believe He's summoning. Summoning His angels for a mighty work, where billions of people are going to be hurt. And this is not the way God really wants it to be, He would much rather you have everlasting life, from here to eternity.

In order to have this, we must change our ways, that is, if you wish to avoid that fiery blaze. He's coming, and I'm truly convinced, in flaming fire, and taking vengeance. II Peter 2:9 "The Lord knoweth how to deliver the godly out of temptations, and to reserve the unjust unto the Day of Judgment to be punished."

Now just to show you how stupid some people are, bless their souls, they think at the end of rainbows, there's a pot of gold. But the rainbow is a covenant, an agreement God made with man; Saying, It wont be water, but fire next time. If you don't believe it, you have to be plum stupid, or totally out of your mind.

Woe unto you who don't believe, Satan has you where he wants, and there's a trick up his sleeve. You see, he's going down, and he refuses to go alone he's whipped! He could never defeat Him who sits on the throne. Yes, Church, he's in misery, and a miserable source indeed, misery loves company, so you best take heed.

II Peter 3:7,8 "But the heavens and earth, which are now, by the same word are kept in store, reserved unto fire against the day of Judgment and perdition of ungodly men. But, Beloved, be not [stupid—"excuse me,"] ignorant of this one thing, that one day with the Lord is as a thousand years, and a thousand years as one day."

The Lord is not slack, and believe me, He's Coming back. What some consider slackness is merely God having patience with us, in hopes we would repent, in the name of Jesus.

II Peter 3:9, The Lord is not slack concerning his promise, as some men count slackness; But is longsuffering towards us, Not willing that any **should perish**, but that **All Should** come to repentance.

Don't Be Stupid, now, **All** will not come to repentance, and this is why His Majesty is preparing sentence. There are a lot of people still in doubt, and I can tell, but a life sentence in heaven, is better than a life sentence in **hell**.

Church, the world is full of stupidity, in your neighborhoods, and immediate vicinity. I say to you, prepare yourselves for the divinity – The Great and the divine, because I tell you now, it's just **a Matter of Time**.

In the Name of Jesus , **Amen.**

Unprotected

As we go through life to and fro... We're not really aware
of where it is we go.
Eating, drinking, and often being merry...
Never realizing **the Burdens We Carry**.
They go on daily feeling things are fine,
Not even aware... "**The Signs of The Times.**"
Famine, pestilence, and rumors of wars...
The world holds on, to those traumatic scars.

But the time is now to draw near to **the Father,**
Although there are those who would say... "Why bother?"
But its time, however, to get closer than close,
The time is at hand for **the Lord of Host**.

Its time to prepare for **The Coming Day**...
You that are burdened it is time to pray.
For you go through life "**unprotected,**"
Only setting yourself up, that is, to be rejected,

To be rejected by **God** is a horrifying thing...
The Fire, His Wrath... "**That Deadly Sting.**"
Its time to get ready, its time to be insured,
Time to resist the devil and stop being lured.

Abstain from being tempted, and yielding to new wave
gadgets,
Or you'll find yourself stepping into something tragic.
We can't go on neglecting **The Light** and saying in our
hearts, Everything is Alright,
Lusting after things and you know are not right, slipping
deeply into the night.

The ways of the world are but a contagious disease,
It's like a chronic cold... it spreads when you sneeze.

Get on board, my friends and avoid being infected...
Let **Jesus** into your life and be protected.
Jesus is **The Key** to one's success...

He's been good to me and I must confess,
I was going through life to and fro,
Looking for pleasures... door to door...
Looking for that which I knew was not right,
Going out with the devil... The Prince of the Night.

Unprotected, I was the devils prey...
Just doing whatever he would say.
I didn't have the strength to make him flee,
The wool was over my eyes; I could not see.

It took a horrifying event to open my eyes,
And what I thought was real, was actually a disguise.
I put myself in a position where only God could deliver,
A frightening situation...It made my whole body quiver.

It's not a good feeling knowing you're about to die,
Caught without Jesus...Failing to comply.
All He asked was to be My Savior,
I rejected Him...for that **Foolish Behavior**.

Life can be perfected if we give God a chance,
And let Him rule in your life...your life He'll enhance,
The fullness of His grace, the mercy He gives...
So that **the Spirit of His Love**, in you, can Live.
Jesus Christ, your personal protection...
The God of Love and of Much affection...

Realize, my friends, what it is you must do,
Stop letting the devil have rule over you.
Start living for God and obey His law...
And He'll do a work in you... He'll remove **The Flaw**.

He'll fill you with **The Holy Ghost**, and make your soul

shout, seasoned Christians know what I'm talking bout.
He'll set fire to your bones, and make you jump to your feet...
He'll make you shake, shiver, and squirm; and come up out of your seat.

He will try you with fire and you'll feel the heat,
He will give you a life that's thorough and complete.
Yes, God will do these things, if you would only allow,
Let Him into your heart... Not tomorrow, Right now!

Don't be **Caught Up** without **Jesus**, that is **Unprotected**,
Accept **Jesus** now and make your life more effective.
The time is near, and it wont be long,
Satan and his army will soon be gone...
Back into the lake, The Lake of Fire.
To be with **Jesus**, should be your hearts desire.

Believe me, church when you are unprotected,
It's when God feels He's been neglected,
And without His protection...Life can be hectic,
And yes, some of us have been infected.

You feel you can conquer this world all alone;
Even world rulers today, they have it all wrong.
Because of their weapons and nuclear power...
What good is it, when you know not the hour?

Like a **Thief in the Night**...Without a fight!
Wake up World, and See the Light.

To deny God's love and His protection, is truly an imperfection,
It puts ones soul in that of subjection.

It's times we left **Jesus**... He didn't leave us,
The security is there, in Him, you can Trust!
So take an in-depth look into your life story...

Going **unprotected**, denies God His Glory.
God is waiting, your life to insure...
Jesus is here to **protect you**; ... to make you Holy and Pure.

Finally... be strong in the Lord and in the Power of His might. Put on the whole armor of God, that you may be able to stand against the wiles of the devil. We do not wrestle against flesh and blood, but against principalities and powers of the devil. We war against rulers of the darkness of this age, and spiritual host of wickedness in high places. Therefore, take the whole armor of God, that you may be able to stand in the evil day... Eph. 6:10-13

Please note, my Christian friends, God feels disrespected, when we choose to go through Life...**unprotected**. **Amen**.

The Hemphill Story

This ain't know crap, this is serious rap, The Hemphill Story...A dreadful mishap.

You see it all had started in Sabine County Jail,
A black man was arrested and he could not make bail.
He was put in a cell all by himself.
And no one heard his cry, as they beat him to death.
There were 3 white men on that Christmas Night,
They tried to say that the black man wanted to fight.
That he was drunk, drugged, and talking out of his head,
And when the dust had settled, The man was dead.

There was a Big Controversy about the whole ordeal,
About what really happened in the town of Hemphill.
The Truth of the matter was left undone,
Because the law men said, that they wasn't the one.

So now the people started talking and charges were filed,
In the case of Loyal Garner, A Civil Rights Trial.
A very good attorney came to his defense,
Which left the whole State in a world of suspense.

The trial went on for days at a time,
Trying to figure out if there was really a crime.
But it's a known fact his rights were violated,
And the verdict will tell if the town is to be hated.

There's a little bit of truth and a whole lotta lies,
As the verdict was read, it was no surprise...
From the jury cause, they already knew,
They hade made up in their minds, their own Point of
View.

Whites against Blacks are on the increase,
A never ending battle as we struggle for peace.
The Jury was selected from the Hometown Folk,
And now they think its over, They Laugh and Joke.

But little do they know, victory is destined to show,
It was a very "Dark Night of the Scarecrow,"
An innocent man who had lost his Breath,
At the hands of the law, They beat and choked him to death.

Another evil killing within the county jail,
Swept under the rug but will it prevail?
"Vengeance is mine, saith the Lord!"
The wicked and the evil are null and void.

The town of Hemphill, Take a look at yourself,
The controversy and verdict that you have left.
Your conscience now shall be your guide,
A brutal murder in Jail you tried to hide.

But what's done in the dark will soon come to the light,
The day will come when we as Blacks will have our Rights.
There's a **Higher Official** (God) And He's looking down on you,
Taking Notes of all the unjust things you do.

The hurt, The Pain, A Son is slain,
The Town of Hemphill is now to blame.
"Its Not Over!" That's what his wife said,
The hands of the Law left her husband dead.

Now she is the widow of one Loyal Garner,
And the way he died will always haunt her.
Like a thief in the night, they took his life,
And all that is left was a grieving wife.

However, the Truth of the matter is a well-known fact,
The man was killed because his color was Black.
The time will come when all is revealed,
That terrible tragedy in the town of Hemphill.

It's a frightening situation, The turn of this nation,
Everything is ran by the White population.
A Black man today He don't stand a chance,
One false move, They will kill you in a glance.

I picked up the paper only to see a sad face,
And the justice handed down by a crooked white race.
You can call it what you want, I do not care,
But the teary-eyed supporters, Their torment you'll share.

A close knit community, a police brutality case,
Another dirty slap to the Black man's race.
When will it stop, Tell me, When will it cease?
Will we The Black Race ever get any peace?

Please Lord Master, Hear the Cry,
The Loyal Garner Family, Please tell us why?
We must suffer at the White man's hand,
The White Supremacist... The Klu Klux Klan.

Caught Up

During my incarceration period, I would often hear offenders make the statement… "The devil put me in prison!" I can't uphold that for the simple reason, the devil's soul purpose is to kill, steal, and destroy. Being incarcerated—to me, lessens the chance of one's demise. I would think that being off the streets, where the devil and his army run rampantly, would somewhat, keep you out of harms way.

For instance, in my situation, I was out of control…Caught Up in the devil's mess. The devil had me so blind until I rebelled against my wife, my pastor… My Lord.

Because of my rebelliousness, I was chastened by God. Oh yes, I've had several spankings and it was only because He loved me. You see, God gave me a gift, and He wanted me to use this gift for His glory that I might draw others into salvation. But for some unearthly reason, I would let the devil disrupt my every thought – my every plan.

On the outside, the free world, I could not stay focused because I couldn't concentrate. I could not hear that small still voice, simply because of the distractions. The temptations, alcohol, drugs, the money, and the women… The wiles of the devil. Only from within these walls was I able to focus. My Mind was clear and more receptive, making it that much easier for God to speak to me. But, when He speaks you have to be willing to hear and be obedient to the Call.

I truly feel my being incarcerated was a "Rescue Mission" set up by God to save me from destruction. I know the devil was trying to kill me, and once he did that, he'd have my soul. It's true, I was about to lose my family, my wife, my kids, business, my mind… My Life. Caught Up…Between right and wrong, I had to make a decision, but because of my addiction, I became weak and unable to think for myself... I was too far gone.

But God made a way for my escape. He put me in a place where I could sit down, recollect my thoughts, look at my pass, and gave me the opportunity to see where I was headed. It has not failed, when it seemed I was headed for a **Dead End**...Traveling at a high rate of speed, God would intervene, Before I careened. In other words, He would save my life.

I'm in this place for a reason and I have God to thank for this. I have a chance now to redeem myself. I have a chance now to turn my life completely around. I have a chance now to turn my life over to **Christ**.

I look at the men who are incarcerated, and who are in church. You can tell who had a relationship with God. You can hear it in a conversation, a song, their testimony, or in a time of sharing. In some way, God had a impact on their lives. You could tell that these men could, or once was, a Soldier for Christ. But something happened, they too apparently got **Caught Up** in Satan's many snares. I'm reminded of the love God showed for us in the story of Job. God told the devil, "You can do as you will to him, but don't kill him!" The devil will, however, attempt to make you kill yourself. The devil told Job's wife to tell him..."Curse God and die."

In all actuality, God wants to use these gifts; the talents that He has so blessed us with. God wants us to draw others into repentance and to be a witness to His mercy, His grace, His Love... His Son; Jesus Christ, who, for our sins paid the ultimate price. Within these walls is the opportunity for restoration, relaxation, and preparation, for a new Nation...The Kingdom of God. It's time for reuniting with our first love and get rooted in **The Word** and become what it is God wants us to Be.

I've had so many opportunities to work for God, I've made a nationwide news broadcast with Channel 13 ABC, The Old Time Religion Radio Station with Dr. Lupo. I've recited inspirations at different churches throughout the State. I've spoke with Publishers, Rodney Gordy with Motown Records and several agency's but not being rooted in **The Word** and in my walk with God, I could not stand...**Caught Up!**

It was from behind these walls was I able to use my gift and to hear God. With all my heart, I believe I was saved from the streets—Saved from destruction. God put me in a place where He could sit me down and talk to me, work on me, heal, deliver, and clean me up. He restored His Spirit in me as well. God wants me to come out this place a strong man, a man of God. A man who can be responsible, who can take care of his family, love his family, and be a role model to the kids. He does not wish that I should perish, but have everlasting life.

Yes, I was **Caught Up** in the ways of the wicked, but as I read my Bible, I find there is no positive future for these people. There is no future in the front. So, its up to me now to take advantage of this restoration period and know what it is I want in life. Truly, there is no life if its not in **Christ**.

What do you do when you get out? Take Christ with you and don't leave Him at the gate. Get into a strong, Spirit-Filled, Full Gospel church and submit to God; Be like a tree planted by the waters, and not be moved.

I think its time now that we use this quality time with God while behind these walls and let Him use us. The days are evil and its time we, as Christians, start to look to the hills from which cometh our strength. It's time we prepare to see the King. Its time we stop playing with God. Stop lying to God and to ourselves, because God is real and will slap the taste from your mouth. Not only that, God will kill you...Dead. Ananias and Sapphira found that out the hard way. **You can't fool God**.

Be real with God and He will be Real with you. **The Rapture is Coming** and in this you want to be **Caught Up** in because **Jesus is Coming** back and we must be ready. That is, if you wish to see a **Brighter**

Day. This is our opportunity to get it right with God, right here, right now. God is coming, He's coming for that church without spot or blemish...We could be that church. I want to be Free...Free from alcohol and drugs, free from anything that's going to keep me out of **The Kingdom of God**. More than anything, **I want to be Caught Up with Jesus**!

Amen.

You've Tried the Rest... Now Try the Best!

A little about distractions a form of deception, "know it when you see it." It's good to see so many people turn out for Christ, people actually turning their lives over to Jesus, who, for our sins, paid a price. So much love has been shown to us, through our Risen Savior, Lord Jesus. How could we not return such love, that God so sent to us from heaven above? The Lord our God loves us, the human race, more than anything He created; I consider this an honor and am truly elated.

In my life I've tried so many things that were of the world and found excitement and enjoyment like any other man, woman, boy, or girl. Things of beauty and of much attraction, unaware that they were only a distraction, Something to amuse me; to get my utmost attention. Deception, trickery, one of Satan's many inventions.

Yes, I've tried them as so many of us have, and sometimes I can hear that old devil as he would laugh. It does him good to capture your soul, anything to keep you from those righteous goals. Oh but he knows he has but a short while, and that's why he wants the soul of every man, woman, and child.

He's really having his way, you can see it in the news each, and every day. Gold and silver at a price, you can afford the bling, but can you take it with you when The Lord calls you aboard? Rolls, Cadillac, man's glory... There's a train a coming, have you heard the story? It'll be picking up passengers from coast to coast leaving behind those who brag and boast. Leaving behind those who glorify their earthly receiving's... Ill-gotten gain as the devil continues his deceiving.

Of course, its something the Lord allows, but because He does, doesn't mean you have to bow...

Rev. 20:2-3..."And he laid hold on the dragon, that old serpent which is the devil, And Satan, and bound him a thousand years, and cast him into the bottomless pit and shut him up and set a seal upon him, that he should deceive the Nation no more till the thousand years should be fulfilled; and after that, he must be loosed a little season. "Deception, my friends, know it when you see it!"

Right now, he's furious, he's mad, he's a loser, and if you really stop to think, he's a user. He uses the good to try and get back at God, but there are some of us who would make that exploitation very hard. I can see him now, a little busy body. He's trying to destroy the lives of everybody, with new and fascinating ideas to get you to try, another deception, yes, another lie!

Woe unto those who inhabit the Earth, for the devil has come unto you with great wrath seeking whom he can devour because he knows he has but a short while. "Deception, know it when you see it!"

Believe me, there's so many ways the devil will come closed caption, but **Jesus** is the Coming Attraction... More action than you can even imagine...for the lost, admission, no cost!

Certainly there are a lot of you who see it the way I do, and know the things I say are true. We can go to the ball games and praise the players, but can't fill the church for **Jesus**, our **Mediator**. It hurts to even think about, the denial of Christ' love we can't live without. We've tried everything practically this world has to offer us, I say its high time now that we try Jesus. We've tried the rest, its time now we try the best, because soon, this old world will be laid to rest...

I don't want to be caught in the stadium worshiping Andre Johnson and the Texans, especially knowing I haven't quite learned my Lesson. Nor do I want to be caught praising Lebron James knowing I'm putting **Jesus Christ** to shame. But to be in the church with Angels, and Saints and don't say you can't because the same opportunity awaits you... Try **Jesus**, it's all you have to do.

Let Satan have his old world full of gadgets and

tricks, its all going soon to the bottomless pit. I know he makes it hard for some of us to leave them alone, but keep this in mind...**Fire and Brimstone**. "The Lake of Fire," be his guest, because if you don't try **Jesus**, you'll join him and the rest.

Rev. 20:10... "And the devil that deceived them was cast into the Lake of Fire and Brimstone, where the beast and the false prophets are and shall be tormented day and night forever and ever, and whosoever was not found written in The Book of Life was cast into **The Lake of Fire."**

Church we've tried the Rest, let's now try the best. If for the rest of your life you want the best, get on the **Jesus** team, and be blessed.

Alpha and Omega (The Beginning, The End, The First, The Last)

In the beginning there was the Heaven and Earth,
This was the creation of a New Birth,
God saw the light and that it was good,
There are many today, who never understood.

The Light was called day, The darkness called night,
The things God does is truly a sight!
The blind made to see and the cripple to walk,
Yet to this day, People still balk.

It's a beautiful Land God made for man,
Why is it so hard to keep His commands?
Praise Him whom we cannot see,
For He gave His life for you and me.

Do God's will and keep His commands,
Let's Save our Souls and move on to the Holy Land.
Because Life is so sweet that He gives to Us,
Praise His name, Lord Jesus!

The things He said that He would do,
Praise God almighty they're about to come true!
For it was told in revelation,
Lest you take heed, its total damnation.

The signs of the times, let's understand,
That which is written, is now at hand!
Thou shall not steal, but we kill,
Knowing all the time its not God's will .

Let's save our souls and make Heaven our goal.
Praise the Lord, for the Bible unfolds,
Kings against Kings, Nations against Nations

The entire world is headed for damnation.

"Blessed is He who is in Me,"
For these are the children who will live eternally.
Famine and wars all over the world,
Lord, Bless the starving babies, Little boys and girls.

Jesus is Precious, Please believe me,
The opportunity awaits for you to be Sin free.
Knock, and the door it shall open,
Let not Satan be your token, where Hell awaits,
But enter into Heaven – The pearly gates.

For Jesus is no liar, but the Holy Messiah.
Take Heed to His Word and avoid the Fire,
Death and destruction, a major eruption
Based on the founder of our corruption.

But put on the whole armor and nothing can harm you.
The things I say, I mean not to alarm you.
Keep your heart pure and you will endure,
In the name of Jesus be Caught Up in the Rapture.

For Jesus is the Alpha and Omega, The First, The Last,
Beginning and the End,
Let's live our lives free of Sin.
For God is the Chancellor and Jesus is the answer,
Lots of prayer will end this cancer.

Words of Wisdom and so very true,
Repent, and God will save you!
Amen.

Whatchha Gonna Do

Bad Boy-Bad Girls, whatcha gonna, whatcha gonna,
whatcha gonna do, when them—come for you?
Nobody gonna give you no break,
Old soldier man will give you no break,
The policeman will give you no break,
And the government will give you no break,

Whatcha Gonna Do Because...
King Jesus's gonna make his break,
Bad Boys, Bad girls, so whatcha gonna do, whatcha gonna do when He comes for you?

Bad Boys—Bad Girls

Yes, brothers and sisters, soon and very soon the heavenly host will arrive, and it's not going to be a pleasant visit for some. I have witnessed things that the Bible says would come to pass, for instance, in the book of Matthew Chapter 24:10 reads: "**And then shall many be offended, and shall betray one another and shall hate one another.**"

During my stay in jail, I was around youth with violent cases, who, when convicted will more than likely be of an old age before they see the outside world again. This is simply because they chose to do wrong, to walk in darkness, gangster style into corruption. As gang members they hardly ever walk alone, indulging in all areas of crime.

When caught, and sooner or later they will be caught, they become confused as to how they got caught when supposedly they had a foolproof plan. Who could have known except those involved? Picture This!

"Say man, how did the police find out? You sold

me out to the man, Bro." "I thought we was down homies. You betrayed me, Homs!"

Hatred then sets in and they began to betray one another to save their own necks by telling off on one another to law enforcement officials for an easier sentence—a lesser time in prison.

To the kids in particular, our boys and girls, if you live a bad life, believe me they will come for you. When you step out of the will of God, you step into corruption, corruption leads to ungodly acts, jail, then prison and or **Death**. I speak to you out of love and experience, because there was a time when I slipped from the hands of the Lord. I was like a little child pulling away from His mother in a toy store to run off to something that attracted me, something that was no good for me. There, I found myself in trouble.

Realizing and hating my mistake, I tried to find my way back; but already the cloud of darkness hovered over me. The troubles, the fear of lock-up, not ready to give up establishing a business. I wanted to do right as the cloud remained. But with prayer; calling upon the Lord, I found someone who would give me a B**reak—Jesus Christ.** I remember Him telling me in Jeremiah 33:3:

"Call unto Me and I will answer thee." Before, I had worried about the business we had established, would Pop be able to go on without me? I had to be cleaned up; thus going into submission, surrendering, allowing the Lord to work on me, and clearing my record with Police officials was a start. Now, the Lord says to me, "I will show you great and Mighty things which thou knowest not."

Right now the Lord is giving most of you a break. Old soldier, man will give you no break. The police man will give you no break, the government will give you no break, but King Jesus will give you a break. So, whatcha gonna do, when they come for you? And tell me, whatcha gonna do when Jesus comes for you? He's coming, He's coming for His church, His people, His children –Boys and girls.

He will also be leaving, leaving behind the wicked bad boys and girls, men and women not in Christ. They will have to face the fervent heat and destruction. It's time to think of those things in heaven and not in earth because the earth is soon to pass away. The Word of God will be Here forever. II Peter 3:10, "But the day of the Lord will come as a thief in the night; in the which the heavens shall pass away with a great noise, and the elements shall melt with fervent heat, the earth also and the **works** that are there in **shall be Burned up**. "

When He comes for you, will you have made peace with the almighty? Will you have shaken off corruption and put on righteousness? Will you have stepped away from those who walk disorderly and not in the Light of God? Will you give up this world to be where He is, to live in His dwelling place? Think on these things boys and girls, children of God. Its time to be sure of where we're going and what we're going to do because **Jesus is Coming. Justice is Coming. Judgments is Coming**. Whatcha gonna do when **They** come for you?

I believe He's preparing His angels to descend upon the earth at any time now; we've had ample warning. In the Old Testament, in the days of Noah the people were really doing it, partying, drinking, and the works. Most of all, they didn't take Noah seriously. For instance, they were aware of Noah building the Ark but didn't Believe, instead they laughed and made fun and even thought he was crazy probably. Well, you can think I'm crazy if you like, but the Lord is moving on me to write and share this message. I'm coming from the New Testament where we're moving into a revealing stage; **A Revelation** where the sins of man **will** be revealed.

We can get caught up in the ways of the World. The enticements of the devil, drugs and alcohol, flirtatious women, fancy cars – cars that go **Boom!** in the night loudly playing music, video games, Nintendo, Sega! Silver and gold we chase. All these things are to distract you from His coming so that you will be caught as in the day of Noah. Not waiting, **not watching, not fighting, nor praying** – not even paying attention to the **works of God.**

Those of us here in the prisons, the Lord is actually giving us a break that we may be free from many of the distractions in the world in hopes we will seek His face. Many don't know how fortunate they are to be alive, to hear some of the stories told. But then, there's ignorance! The Lord is warning us daily, He's truly giving us a break. It's all coming to pass, and fast. The signing of the peace treaty.

I'm asking the church, what are we gonna do? Believe me its getting close with all my heart I believe this to be the generation. It has to be the upcoming generation because we can't get off the ground. They are killing one another, **Our Kids**. Actually destroying themselves with drive by shootings, gangs, and this is very serious! The youth today are armed and dangerous. It's time to prepare those who will hear; who have not tasted the world, prepare them for **The Coming of The Lord**. The Lord has been good; He's been merciful, pitiful, longsuffering, patient, and simply beautiful. It's high time we let the Holy Ghost have His way in our lives, it is time to resist the devil – **Not the Holy Spirit!**

So, Again I ask, whatcha gonna do? When Jesus Comes for you?

The Preacher

I went to church one morning and was happy in what I saw and heard. You see, **The Preacher** was in the pulpit, dancing and shouting The Word. He said, "I feel real happy in what I have to say today." He went on to say, "**Jesus is here**, and He's leading me on this day. Again He Said, Jesus –Jesus is here church, and He's given me these words to say. "Now I've got a **message** for you, direct from His majesty's throne, and He's saying, "Come home children **It's Time** for you **To Come Home**!"

Hello to all, and to all I say, "**Thank God** for **Ecclesiastes, The Preacher**." Yes, the preacher, a servant of the Lord, a minister, a messenger, a shepherd, a disciple, a person anointed of God. He's inspired by His Holy Spirit to Preach, teach and beseech us all to become aware of the Lord God Almighty, **Jesus Christ**.

I come not to condemn nor pass judgment on anyone, but to say through hearing the word as administered by one of God's chosen preachers, I've learned you will know the righteous by the fruit they bear. I've learned that the Spirit will bear witness to itself. I've learned to respect the Word of God.

I come today to lift up The Preacher because he is sent of God and is anointed. Believe me, The Lord will work with him hand in hand. Today, there is much work to be done; there is a harvest to be reaped. "There isn't much time, church!" The Preacher might say to those who hear what he has to say to the church, because The Preacher is also one who is under instruction. His instructions come from the Lord and thus handed down to us, the church.

The preacher is commissioned by God and licensed to speak to you with boldness and in authority. A true Preacher, mind you. God will back him 100% to them who believe in Jesus, and the power of God. If you will, read Mark 16:15-20, It reads like this:

"And He said unto them, (the disciples), "Go ye unto all the world, and preach the Gospel to every creature. He that believeth and is baptized shall be saved; but He that believeth not shall be damned. And these signs shall follow them that believe; In my name shall they cast out devils; they shall speak with new tongues; They shall take up serpents; and if they drink any deadly thing, it shall not hurt them; they shall lay hands on the sick; and they shall recover. So then, after the Lord had spoken unto them, He was received up into heaven, and sat on the right hand of God. And they (The Preachers) went forth, and preached everywhere, the Lord working with them, and confirming the Word with signs following. "Amen?" Amen.

Don't you just Love good preaching? I love to hear the Word of God, especially coming from an anointed man of God, or woman for that matter. The Words have a tendency to stick, to get inside you like fire shut up in your bones, causing a Holy Ghost reaction. It makes you want to get up out your seat and dance and shout, extending praises unto the Lord; believe me, He loves this! The Holy Spirit is real and He lives within you.

I love good preaching! I love for The Preacher to put a Holy smile on my face. I love for the preacher to lift my countenance, to reassure me of God's tender mercy, His love, and His forgiving heart. I love for The Preacher to tell me, "Its time for me to get ready, get ready for the harvest, ready for the Kingdom, for the end is nigh to thee." I love verse 20 of Mark 16, And they went forth, and Preached Everywhere the Lord Jesus Christ, He was working with them, as they carried the Gospel throughout the world; He worked with them not by Might, Nor by power, but by His Spirit. Yes, Jesus was going back up to His throne, His seat, at the right hand of God and substantiating the words they, as preachers, stood and delivered with signs and wonders.

I say to you church, love the Lord, and love the Preacher, for He is indeed Ecclesiastes. He knows what time it is, and he knows because he is in close communication with the Holy Spirit. He's under instruction and is instructed to preach to you salvation that you may be saved from eternal damnation and used for that of the Kingdom, "The Last Harvest."

The Holy Spirit is speaking to me now as I read the Morning paper that reads, "Court Orders Judgment Day for Preacher." Church, let not these things hinder your congregation, nor come among you, bickering causing confusion, doubting your pastor's guidance. Instead, support the preacher who shepherds you who watches over you, your life, your safety, because without the proper guidance and instructions, you too could be headed for destruction.

I could go on and on as the Spirit leads me, but let me say that the Lord will pour out His Spirit upon all flesh; on every creature, the Word must be preached everywhere, and there's none better qualified than your Preacher.

In the Name of Jesus. Amen. The Final Note in consideration of "**The Harvest**" let me share these words from Mark 4:26,29

"And he said, so is the kingdom of God as if a man should cast seed into the ground; and should sleep, and rise night and day, and the seed should spring and grown up, he knoweth not how. For the Earth Bringeth forth Fruit of herself; First the blade, then the ear, after that the fall corn in the ear. **But** when the fruit is brought forth, immediately, he putteth in the sickle, because **The Harvest is Come**."

Be Ready For The Harvest. May God Bless you all. Amen.

They Shall Know "I am the Lord"

Church family, friends, saints, the Lord God is expounding heavy in my heart a message. This message of repentance is strong. If you think you can continue to go through life getting away with murder, just doing whatever you want, I must tell you there are consequences some painful, some tragic. I ask you, have you not seen or endured enough tragedy?

My heart bleeds for those who do not know the Lord God Jehovah, but God has informed me there is Hope for those whose life or lives are scarred. People, we must come to grips with ourselves, this world is about to be dissolved. There are atoms God has stored up for the Coming Day and they are about to be released.

A consuming fire that's going to dissolve the earth and heaven. There will be a new heaven, a new earth. Read about in 2 Peter 3:10. But if you really want to know what's happening go to Rev. 20. This world is on the way to disaster and soon all will know who is the master. Remember, it won't be water but fire next time.

Look at the wars taking place, the terrorism the hatred, the animosity between nations, families, and friends...Saints of God. We're in devastating times and it seems no one is listening or paying attention to what God is doing. He's unleashing His anger daily, His wrath is terrible.

Church, Let me tell you about "**The Great I am**." It's time to wake up and recognize what we're doing with what life God has given us, and stop denying **Jesus**. Its time to understand that we're dealing with a power that has the power over life and death, who when you awake gave you breath. There's a lot of people who did not wake up this morning, the ones who loved them now in mourning. Church its time to Know, its time to **know** the maker, the creator.

Church family, friends, saints of God in the Lord, when He said He's going to do something believe it! Something's that take place in our lives are but for our on good and chastisement, discipline, we need it. If we were not disciplined or chasten from above, this would mean there is no **Love**. If we as children don't respect our mother, father, or stepfather, and keep doing that which is wrong, your days are numbered and surely it wont be long.

When you leave that mighty hand, its then, you will know why things are not working out for you as planned. You will **know** in this life where you stand. (with Christ who paid the price) The Lord, Trust me He is not a coward, and for you who think He is, then you look forward to a day of reckoning.

Believe me, the Lord is becoming frustrated and I like Peter am becoming to hate it. He is upset church and its hard for Him to shake it. Sooner or later, we as a sinful nation, a sinful people, will cause God to show His hand. You remember Noah and what He did to the land? **Jesus** is alive and **Just**, and He will wash His hands of us. If you don't know, truly don't know, who he is stay in His Word and He will bottle your tears.

Dear people whom I love, I speak to you out of love, and my thoughts, inspirations, messages come from. Above, the Holy Spirit, wants you to hear it. We have to be inspirations to other sisters and brothers, of who He is and what He's capable of doing. Above all things, He does not want to see our lives in ruin. But He does want to see you repent of your sins, even me, and trust me, I want to make it in.

Jesus wants to be your friend but unless we repent, forgive and forget, and recognize who He has sent, our hopes, dreams, and desire, up in smoke they went. You have to understand, and in all your getting, get that understanding. For the Lord who created everything, He created evil and He will bring evil on you...Let me help you. So it's a must that we change from what evil men do.

Jeremiah 18:8-10 ..."If that nation, that people, against whom I have pronounced, Turn from their evil, I will repent of the evil, (you see, The Lord even repents) that I thought to do unto them. Verse 10, if it do evil in my sight, that it obey not my voice, and that could be my voice, trust me He's working in me. Then I will repent of the good, wherewith I said I would benefit them."

A lot of you expecting something you should have already had, but the evil you harbor holds you up. The Lord is good but He's also tough, its really up to us if we are to change. I'm just informing you, He's had **Enough**! Believe me, He's about to show, that you will know who He is and whom. You will not overthrow.

Take heed to these words church, they too are inspired of God. Jeremiah, as I end, 16:21 and it reads..."Therefore, behold, I will this once cause them to **know**, I will cause them to know mine hand and my might; and they shall know, that my name is the Lord."

In the name of **Jesus** in whom my inspirations come for the glorification of God.

Amen.

The Love of A Baby Sister... We Never Had a Clue

The youngest of them all, who apparently heard the call, but who knew, we never had a clue. We would always look around, but baby sister was nowhere to be found,
For some reason she couldn't get it right, until one night, with the devil she had to put up a fight. Now we wonder is baby sister alright? I can see her from an angle and she would always appear as an angel. But who knew, we never had a clue.

Baby sister would always say, no pain, no gain, my life is destine for change. When you see her she would have this blushing smile, that only lasts for a while. Her big brown eyes always looking around, but in her face, in her face she just wanted to be found. But who knew, we never had clue. She had fell to the ground, I mean all they way down, and yet surfaced, to turn her life around, no more underground.

Her heart filled with love and kindness, for she saw good in everyone and always wanted to help, but who knew, we never had a clue as to how she felt. Looking at it today, baby sister was searching for love too. As I watch my baby sister grow, it showed me more of who she was, a baby sister just looking for love. A few years went by, nothing seemed to catch her eye, but who knew, we never had a clue.

Now understand, I just wished I had extended a hand to catch her before she fell. But through it all, she now has a testimony to tell. I understand her now, and extend all my love to her because she has shown me the love of a baby sister. She was lost but now she's found, and now Jesus has added a jewel to her crown. We just never knew, never had a clue. When you desire to be different, never let anyone treat you the same, let Jesus be your claim to fame.
In loving memory of my loving sister, Michelle Y. Gray.

"A Sister's Testimony"

Bow Down

Looking through my window, I am six stories up, I see a world on the run, of children who are corrupt.
I see a people who are lost and in a land of mass confusion, battered and mangled body; multiple contusions.
I see mother's dying and baby's crying, I see daddy's on the run responsibilities denying. I see violence and crime at a all time high. I can hear our ancestors as they cry.
I see our youth dying daily in gang land war, and those that aren't killed, end up behind bars—in a dispute over power, colors, and that turf, just another of many reasons why Jesus Christ is coming back to earth.

I see a people who think life is nothing but a game. I see a people who never once called upon His name. I see people worship Him, but yet are ashamed. I see Jesus touching lives and no more are they the same. There's coming a time my friend, when the Northside, Eastside, Southside, and Westside, every knee in every single town, will have no option but to bow down. I say to you now, come to the Lord before it is too late, for you are appointed a time; you do have a date. No man knows the date, the time, nor the hour, that Jesus is coming back with vengeance and in power. What will you do when the sky splits and the trumpets sound?

You can't run; you can't hide. You've got to bow down. For every knee shall bow and every tongue confess. Come to the Lord if you want to be blessed. Jesus is Lord and by no other name can you be saved. **Judgment is coming** on how you behave. If you haven't made peace with our Lord Jesus Christ, now is the acceptable time, or you'll pay a price. Come to the alter and add a jewel to your crown. Come before His presence and willfully bow down.

About the Author

A native of Ohio, born in Dayton but reared in a small town called Spring, TX is where I became aware of my writing talent. My English Teacher discovered this gift I had and encouraged me to pursue it. In my later years, my life took a turn because I had made some poor decisions. Those decisions caused me to have to take a leave of absence from my family.

During this time away, I had a spiritual encounter where God showed me something's, and in a way that would change my life. God had blessed me to do a nation-wide broadcast from inside the walls with ABC News, A Sports News Exclusive. Since that overwhelming experience, I vowed to write for the Lord, and become a creative writer lifting up the name of Jesus.

Now, I am a devout Christian and member of New Creation Cathedral Church of Houston Texas under the leadership of Bishop Anthony and and first Lady Brenda Mosley, who have been very supportive of this book. This book, Up Close and Personal: Poetically Speaking... has been compiled with testimonies and inspirations given me by God, designed to encourage Hearts and Minds to take a closer walk with thee.

If you like to read pros or poerty, there is something in this book for you to read and be encouraged by. I am also planing to release more books in the future as well as other writings as the Lord is constantly pouring into me and it is my mission to pour that Good News Ou

Order books from William Gray and other published authors at KLEPub.com or where Books are sold! Get E-books only at KLEPub.com

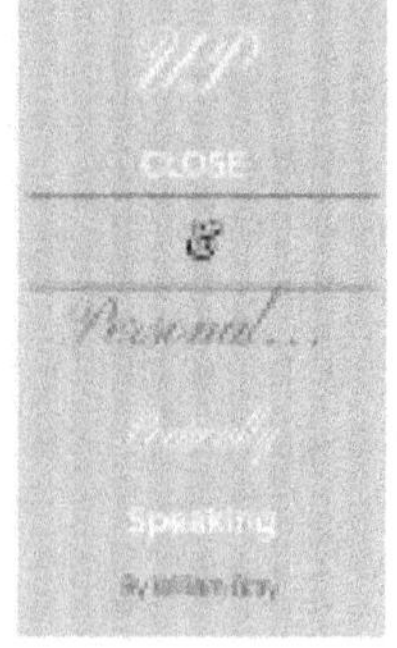

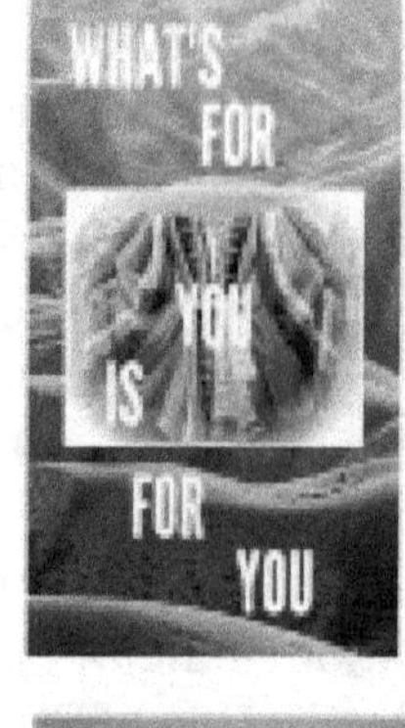

www.ingramcontent.com/pod-product-compliance
Lightning Source LLC
Chambersburg PA
CBHW070444170726
48291CB00005B/1598

* 9 7 8 1 9 4 5 0 6 6 0 0 9 *